I0691609

RELUCTANT DATE

By Sheila Claydon

Amazon Print 978-1-77362-744-1

Books We Love
A quality publisher of genre fiction.
Airdrie Alberta

Copyright 2012 by Sheila Claydon
Cover Art by Michelle Lee

Dedication and Acknowledgements

For Michael
Who knows Dolphin Key....

Chapter One

Claire pulled off her hat and shook out her hair as she glanced around the hotel foyer. There was no sign of anyone who looked like her date for the evening but she had gotten used to that. She was also resigned to the fact that a lot of the men who signed up to dating agencies seemed to have an inflated view of their own attraction. It hadn't taken her long to realize *tall and well built* was a code for big and overweight and *relaxed and informal* was the wrong side of scruffy. She had also discovered that any reference to an unusual hobby almost always meant obsessive.

She found a comfortable chair and settled down to wait. Fifteen minutes she would give him. After that she was out of here, the crazy challenge she'd accepted at a tedious New Year's party over and done with.

* * *

"Twelve dates unless we get lucky," Jenny said as they pushed their way out of the cramped restroom in the over-hyped nightclub where they were celebrating.

Claire's partner for the evening had so little personal charisma she didn't immediately recognize him again when she climbed the dark and treacherous stairs back up to the dance floor. Reluctantly accepting the fact that her personal life had hit an all time low, she threw caution to the wind and agreed to take up the challenge.

Jenny, who had organized their disastrous double date in a fog of depression brought on by her approaching birthday, had tried to pass some of the blame for the evening onto Claire as they washed their hands.

"Honestly, I don't know what else you expect," she shouted above the heavy drumbeat that was threatening to bring down the ceiling. "You work in a library all week and then spend most of your free time taking photographs. You're never going to find a man that way Claire, unless he's a complete loser that is!"

"I know some very nice losers," Claire replied with a grin. "Take my boss for instance."

Jenny rolled her eyes in disgust. "It doesn't make him marrying material though, does it? Why else is he still living with his mother? He must be at least fifty."

Claire stopped thinking about John, her very nice but very eccentric boss, and stared at Jenny's reflection in the dingy mirror. "Who says I'm looking for a husband?" she asked.

"I do! Face it Claire. We're both pushing twenty-seven and here we are doing the same things we were doing at seventeen. It can't go on much longer or we'll begin to look like a couple of real saddos."

"Speak for yourself," Claire repaired her lipstick with unnecessary energy. "I happen to like my life, and we're *not* doing the same things we were doing ten years ago, well not as often anyway. I live a blameless existence most of the time. It's only when you decide to act as my dating agency that I have any problems."

And that was when Jenny had come up with her plan.

"That's it!" she gasped. "We'll join an Internet Dating Agency. We'll find some real men, men who are looking for commitment just like us."

"I told you, I'm not looking for commitment," sighed Claire as, with a final glance at her reflection, she directed her friend towards the doorway. "All I want is to get this evening over with so I can go home. Alone. And go to bed."

But Jenny wasn't listening. "I can't imagine why we haven't thought of it before," she said as they returned to their table. "After all anything must be better than this!"

Claire, who had already spent a large part of the evening dancing as far away from her date as she could manage, could only agree. So, as the clock ticked on to midnight, and the noise levels in the nightclub climbed several more decibels, she accepted the challenge Jenny shouted into her ear. Signing up to an Internet Dating Agency would be her New Year's resolution.

* * *

That, however, had been then. Now, almost ten months later, she had just about had it. To be fair not all of the men had been bad. A couple had been okay. She had even agreed to a second date with one of them because they read the same books, liked the same music and enjoyed the same films. Smiling agreeably, she had persuaded herself that compatibility was a good enough starting point. When he suggested they meet for a third time, however, she had turned him down, because by then she was bored enough to know she didn't care if she never saw him again.

All of which had led her to the here and now, waiting for a stranger in a hotel foyer while she watched the world go by. The problem was it had worked for Jenny. On her sixth date she had met Mark and she was now four months into a blissful affair that showed every sign of long-term commitment. Unfortunately the fulfillment of her own dreams had not stopped her from worrying about Claire's single state. If anything, it had made her worse.

"If it can happen to me, then it can happen to you," she insisted when they met up for a drink after work. "You're far more attractive than me, and more intelligent. The problem is you're not taking it seriously; and you have to unless you want to end up an embittered old spinster."

Claire spluttered into her wine. "Excuse me! The embittered old spinsters, as you so quaintly describe them, are today's feisty, independent and adventurous singletons. We live in the twenty-first century now, in case you haven't noticed."

But Jenny was too wrapped up in her own version of romantic bliss to listen. Wanting each new date to turn out to be Claire's 'Mister Right,' she spent a lot of time trying to persuade her friend she needed to adopt a better attitude.

Finally, thoroughly exasperated, Claire lost her temper. "I'm not what they're expecting," she snapped. "My profile says tall and slim which instantly translates into potential model material to most men, so when they meet a six foot Amazon with big feet they're not impressed."

"Rubbish!" snapped Jenny, equally exasperated. "You're just afraid of commitment, afraid of settling down, and so you keep looking for excuses. The reason hardly any of your dates has asked to meet up again is because they can sense that you're not serious. To you this is just a big joke."

"Oh for goodness' sake," Claire swallowed the last of her wine and pushed back her chair in disgust. "Internet dating isn't about men asking women out. It's about mutual attraction; the freedom for women, as well as men, to chose. So far I haven't met a single man I would waste a second date on, let alone give him house room!"

"Well maybe you're just too picky!" Jenny drained her own glass, and then went all misty eyed as Mark pushed open the door. When he saw her, his face lit up. Thoroughly irritated by her conversation with Jenny, Claire gave them both a cool nod and left them to it.

* * *

Now, however, waiting for her twelfth and final date, she wondered if Jenny was right. Perhaps her past experiences *had* made her too picky. Maybe she was waiting for something that would never happen. Maybe it was time she gave up expecting Prince Charming and began to consider the frogs. That was assuming she wanted to consider anyone at all of course.

Irritated with thoughts that brought back uncomfortable memories, she glanced at her watch. Seven-thirty! It was already fifteen minutes beyond her self-imposed deadline so it was time she got out of here and got on with the rest of her life. As far as she was concerned a 'no show' counted just as much as a flesh and blood date. Now she could retire from the Internet dating scene with her honour intact. She bundled her thick black curls back into her woollen hat and bent to retrieve her bag. When she straightened up a very tall man was standing in front of her with a look of embarrassed apology on his face.

"Claire Harris?" he asked.

Bemused, she nodded. This wasn't Daniel Marchant, her date. He was too old for one thing, and too tired, and too serious. And yet, as she searched his features, she saw there was a resemblance. It was as if he were a sepia image of the real thing. He had the same eyes, the same mouth, even the same hair although it was longer. He just didn't have the colour and animation of the photo he had posted on the agency website.

"You're going?" he said it as a question. He had an American accent.

"Yes, and I don't usually wait this long," she replied, her tone and her expression equally frosty.

"I don't blame you but I would be glad if you would stay for a moment longer, so I can explain."

"There's nothing to explain. We arranged to meet at seven. I was on time. You were late. End of story."

"Not quite I'm afraid. You see I didn't arrange to meet you. My brother organized our date and then left a message on my voicemail, a message I have only just discovered."

Claire's face flushed a dull red. It was bad enough going through this charade because of a stupid New Year's challenge without ending up with someone who couldn't even be bothered to arrange his own dates. She drew herself up to her full height.

"If you think that makes it better Mr Marchant then you know nothing about women.

11

Doesn't your brother mind acting as your, your…agent?" She bit back several of the more descriptive words that sprang to mind.

Daniel Marchant stood his ground. "Unfortunately not! He sees it as his life's work. He has a nice wife who is recently pregnant and I think that must be what has triggered this…uh…fiasco!"

It was clear he considered he owed her a full explanation but, as he spoke, the expression on his face was one of weary resignation.

"Carl is younger than me, so my ongoing single state while he settles into impending fatherhood offends his romantic view of how the world works Miss Harris. And now I've rejected the last of his available female friends he has obviously decided to move things up a notch. Unfortunately he did it without informing me at any point along the way."

His voice, as he explained the situation, was full of irritation. He also looked very tired. Claire knew she should feel sorry for him but for some unaccountable reason she suddenly wanted to laugh. Her lips twitched as she struggled to control herself.

He gave her a sharp look. "Unlike me, you seem to find the situation amusing Miss Harris."

"Call me Claire, please," she managed, before going into a paroxysm of giggles that rendered her entirely speechless for several seconds. By the time she finally calmed down Daniel Marchant had stopped glaring although he wasn't quite ready to smile.

"Sorry," she said, still gasping for breath. "I'm not laughing *at* you. Well…not *just* at you! It's me too. We've both let other people call the shots which, given that we are mature adults, is totally ridiculous. I'm only here because my friend challenged me to join an Internet Dating Agency. She said I needed to find a husband."

"And do you?"

"You know I really don't," she said. "This has made me realize I'm quite happy with my life as it is, even if I am in a bit of a rut. Perhaps I'll just change my job instead, or book an exotic holiday or something."

He smiled then. "A much safer bet Claire Harris."

She grinned at him, hoisted her bag onto her shoulder, and held out her hand. "This has been my best date bar none. As well as making me laugh it has made me see sense. I don't want a husband. I don't even want a date. I should never have listened to my friend."

His smile grew wider. "Now we have established neither of us is remotely interested in marriage, or even dating, how about joining me for a meal? I can't guarantee that I'll be good company because jet lag is bound to kick in shortly. I would like to make up for my brother's crass behaviour though, if you'll let me."

"Won't that just encourage him?" Claire was still chuckling.

"Not if I don't tell him, it won't. Come on. Let's see what the hotel bistro has to offer. I'm afraid I'm not up to anything more exciting than that this evening."

* * *

Ten minutes later, crammed into an alcove designed for people with much shorter legs, Daniel Marchant raised a glass of red wine to his mouth with a wry smile.

"Here's to the single life."

Claire laughed as she picked up her own glass. "Now we've established that we don't need to impress one another, I want to know exactly how long ago that photo of you was taken."

He looked confused for a moment until he realized she was referring to the photo on the Dating Agency web site. Then he gave a resigned shrug. "As I didn't know I'd signed up until half an hour ago, I haven't looked at my profile. I would guess it flatters me though."

"You had shorter hair," she told him. "And you were very tanned."

"If I was laughing and wearing the sort of white T-shirt that had me looking like an all American college boy, then I'll kill myself!"

She grinned as she gave a slow nod. "Will I get to watch?"

"No, because on second thoughts I think I'd rather kill my brother! That photo is at least eight years old."

"He was only following the rules. I haven't met anybody yet who looks like his photo, well not much like it anyway. One guy even went from a shoulder length curls to shaved head in the interval between initial contact and our meeting."

Daniel gave her a quizzical look. "What about you?"

"I submitted the best one I had. You know, full make-up, the works, but it did look like me…at least I think it did. Maybe once my dates saw me in the flesh they were disappointed too."

"I doubt that very much," he said, and the way he looked at her as he lifted his glass to his lips brought a sudden flush of colour to Claire's normally pale face.

At that moment the waiter arrived with a laden tray. By the time he had unloaded it she had persuaded herself that the brief flash of admiration she had seen in Daniel Marchant's eyes was a figment of her imagination. She had also persuaded herself to ignore the fact that they were a deep brown with long lashes, and were set wide apart under straight brows.

She shook away a fluttery feeling stirring deep inside her. A feeling that seemed to have been ignited by his level gaze, and by the husky drawl of his voice. Anxious to distract herself, she asked him about his jet lag.

He shrugged, cutting into his steak. "It goes with the job," he said. Then, before Claire could question him further, he began to ask her about her own life.

* * *

They were halfway through coffee before Daniel Marchant's increasingly stifled yawns prompted Claire to glance at her watch. With an exclamation of horror she drained her cup and pushed back her chair. She had been keeping him from his bed for hours.

"I'm so sorry!" she said, gathering up her bag. "I didn't realize it was this late. You should have reminded me about the jet lag."

He stood up too, and helped her into her coat. "You've done me a favour by keeping me awake. With any luck I'll sleep through until early morning now."

Claire gave him a doubtful smile. She knew he was just being polite. How could she have been so thoughtless? It wasn't as if he had actually wanted to have dinner with her in the first place. She held out her hand.

"Thank you for the meal. I really enjoyed it. Don't be too hard on your brother either. He's just looking out for you."

Although he smiled at her, he made no attempt to take her hand. "Maybe you're right. Maybe just this once I'll let him off the hook because I've enjoyed myself too. Now let's see if someone at reception can rustle up a taxi for you."

"Don't be silly. It's only a couple of stops on the bus."

"Nonsense! It's dark and it's raining, and even though we are reluctant dates I still need to make sure you get home safely."

Her eyes widened. Looks, manners, and now chivalry. Too taken aback to argue she let him shepherd her towards the foyer, and then waited obediently while he organized a taxi. Within moments the doorman indicated that one had arrived. Minutes later she was being driven through streets slick with rain, her hurried thanks to Daniel Marchant a fading memory.

* * *

Daniel leaned wearily against the elevator as it carried him upwards. *Why now? Why her?*

If Carl hadn't interfered he would have remained perfectly content with his life and with his hard won equilibrium. It had taken him years to get there. Years of family trauma, and years of running an organisation that held little interest for him so college fees and medical bills could be paid. He had found a way, too, of balancing his own interests with earning the money needed to keep the family afloat. He had also persuaded himself that a single and single-minded life was a necessary state if he was to achieve everything he wanted. And now, Claire!

One look into her cool gray eyes was all it had taken. That, and her infectious laughter! It had only gotten worse when he noticed the luminosity of her pale skin, the shots of violet in her cloud of black curls, and the long, long legs encased in tight jeans. Without wanting to he had found himself falling deeper and deeper into the hole where he had once had a heart. And getting to know her better hadn't helped. All that had done was open up the ache of loneliness he had hidden from himself for a very long time.

Talking to Claire, sitting opposite her, watching the expressions change on her mobile face had just made him want to know her more. But he was out of luck because from the very first minute they met she had made it abundantly clear she wasn't remotely interested in settling down. Meeting someone and falling in love was quite obviously the last thing on her mind.

Chapter Two

Searching in her purse for change Claire didn't notice the taxi driver getting out of the car until he opened the passenger door, exposing her to the harsh glare of the street light.

"It's been paid for already luv," he said, waving away her proffered coins. "Gentleman said I was to make sure you got home safe. Told me to walk you to your door."

A bubble of laughter threatened again as Claire scrambled out of the cab. He was at least four inches shorter than her, and by the time he had climbed the steps up to her apartment he'd developed a wheezing cough. Some Sir Galahad!

He seemed to see the funny side of the situation himself because he grinned at her as she unlocked her door. "It's earned me a good tip," he said by way of explanation as he turned back to his car.

Closing the door behind her, Claire dumped her bag and hat on the table. Then, without pausing to remove her coat, she hurried across to her computer and switched it on. Within moments she had logged into the Dating Agency site but when she searched for Daniel Marchant there were no matches for his name.

She sat back in her chair, ignoring the two emails in her message box. He had deleted his profile already. Not that she was actually interested in seeing him again. She just wanted to read his details because she had learned very little about him during their meal. He'd told her he worked in tourism, and said he travelled a lot, but apart from that he hadn't told her anything else at all. And now it was too late.

It was her own fault for not doing her homework. Once she realized most prospective dates exaggerated their profiles she'd lost interest in actually checking out anything but the most basic information, preferring to rely on a face-to-face meeting for the truth. Consequently she knew next to nothing about Daniel Marchant. She'd only agreed to meet him because she needed a final date, he had asked her, and he looked good.

Except he hadn't asked her of course! It had been his brother Carl. And during the meal Daniel had kept their conversation concentrated on Claire. He'd asked about her job and what she did in her spare time and, flattered by his interest, she had found herself telling him about her work and then about her photography. She'd even told him that her long-term dream was to find a job where she could combine her library training with her camera skills.

Now, reflecting on their conversation, she was amazed she'd told him so much. She was normally fairly reserved with strangers and yet, somehow, Daniel Marchant had coaxed most of the details of her life out of her. He knew she was a librarian. He also knew she was an only child, and that her parents had been quite old when they had her.

"They're still old hippies," she had explained with a laugh as she related a few outlandish anecdotes from her childhood. "They've always been so alternative and eccentric that I more or less brought myself up. They never really told me what to do. That's probably why I've ended up working in a library. I'm sure a psychologist would say it's some sort of inner bid for order after the chaos of my upbringing."

He had laughed with her, but the wistful note in his voice hadn't escaped her. "Very different from my childhood then," he'd said. "I come from a deeply conservative and buttoned up sort of family with rules for everything."

And now she would never know. Her only way of contacting him had been via the website message box because nobody with any sense gave out their telephone number or address. Instead, they saved such personal details for later, for when they were sure they wanted to meet again. So now she couldn't even thank him for the meal because he had chosen to take himself off the market before he went to bed. Not that she blamed him. She was going to do exactly the same thing. The sooner she forgot about the fiasco of her affair with the Internet, and particularly her brief encounter with Daniel Marchant, the better.

* * *

The rest of the week dragged. Not even the prospect of a visit from a class of primary school children raised Claire's spirits. Normally she enjoyed showing them how the library worked and asking about their favourite stories. Days before they were due she would choose bookmarks, prepare quiz sheets, and download colouring pictures from the Internet. Then she would search for a book of the right length so she could read them a ten-minute story at the end of their visit. This time, however, she found everything a chore.

By Friday morning, the cheerful middle-aged women who worked with her had started looking at her with worried expressions. She forced a smile and assured them she was fine. And she was fine except…except she couldn't get the memory of Daniel Marchant out of her head.

"I just need a change of scene," she told them. "Some fresh air. A walk along the beach."

"You'll be going to visit your parents then?" they said.

She nodded. That was exactly what she would do. She knew she was always welcome at the big rambling house her parents had bought when their advancing years had finally persuaded them to settle down. Old and battered, it took the full brunt of the northwest wind that blew with varying degrees of force for most of the year, but she loved it. She visited often because it was close to the sea, and to a nature reserve full of the things that she loved to photograph.

If she finished work early there would just be enough time to go home, throw jeans and a sweater into a bag, and catch the six o'clock train.

Happier now she had something to look forward to instead of mooning around all weekend pretending Daniel Marchant hadn't happened, she checked the time. As she did so the double doors burst open and a class of solemn seven-year-olds came in followed by a harassed teacher and two classroom aides.

Claire smiled at them and told them to pile their coats and hats onto one of the reading benches well away from the busier part of the library. Then she led them through to the children's section. For the next hour she answered questions and talked about books. Not until she finished reading the final page of the story she had chosen did she remember a leaflet that had arrived with the morning's post.

"Who likes poetry?" she asked.

Twenty-four hands shot into the air.

"Good, because I've the very thing for all of you. A poetry competition! I'll photocopy the details for your teacher while you collect your belongings."

She was smiling as she led them back into the main library, a smile that faded into a look of total disbelief when she saw Daniel Marchant standing there. Something about the way he was leaning against the counter told her he had been waiting for quite sometime.

"Hello," his eyes had golden flecks that she didn't remember. He didn't smile.

"I…I…what are you doing here?"

"Looking for you. It's taken me quite a while to track you down."

He didn't look tired now, and without the shadows under his eyes he was even more attractive than the first time she met him. Something inside her that might have been her heart, shifted slightly. She pulled herself together. She was at work and Daniel Marchant wasn't interested in dating. He had made that very clear when they met.

"Just let me finish what I'm doing and then I'll take an early lunch break," she said. Then she ignored the knowing look that Elsie gave her and did her best to concentrate on photocopying the poetry leaflet.

* * *

Ten minutes later they were hurrying across the road to the local sandwich shop, their heads down against a sudden squall of rain. Claire pushed open the door and Daniel followed her inside.

"This wasn't quite what I had in mind," he said with a wry nod towards the huge chalkboard that listed the day's sandwich fillings.

"Sorry, but I've arranged to have a short lunch break today so I can leave at four o'clock. I'm going to visit my parents," she added as she studied the chalkboard and wondered why she didn't feel hungry.

Once they had collected their order she grabbed a table well away from the door so they wouldn't be interrupted by the steady flow of people who were ordering food to take out.

"Why are you here?" she said. It came out more forcefully than she intended because she didn't for one moment think Daniel Marchant was a stalker. Nor was he a weirdo, or an eccentric, or any of the other things she had learned to avoid when she arranged her dates.

He held up his hands in silent apology for his unannounced intrusion into her working day. "I've come to offer you a job," he said.

Whatever Claire had expected, it wasn't that. She stared at him in disbelief.

He smiled at her bemused expression. "You did say you were in a rut and maybe a solution was to change your job," he reminded her.

She nodded. While half of her was intrigued by the prospect of something so unexpected happening to her, the other half felt deflated. So he hadn't come searching because he wanted another date. No! It was because he had a job vacancy and she fitted. Remembering how skillfully he had uncovered all the details of her life as they chatted over their shared meal, something sharp twisted in her heart.

Daniel Marchant had been interviewing her. He wasn't interested in her personally at all.

"Don't you want to know what it is?" he asked.

"I suppose so," she knew she sounded grudging but it was difficult not to when her head was warring with her heart, and her heart was winning.

"I run a small company involved in coastal research and I need someone to photograph and catalogue the results of the work we are doing."

Claire's eyes widened. "It sounds interesting but why me?"

"Because you have the right qualifications and, unless my memory has failed me, an keen interest in wildlife. You also told me you thought travelling or a new job might be what you needed. If you decide to take the job, you can do both."

"Well yes, but...did you say travelling?"

"Mmm," Daniel spoke around a mouthful of sandwich. He swallowed it. "The job is in Florida."

Claire stared at him. She was lost for words. Florida! A dream job in Florida, and all she could think of was that Florida was a long way away and she didn't know anything about him. The jumble of thoughts loosened her tongue.

"Your profile said you work in tourism."

" I do," he pushed the plate of sandwiches towards her. "As well as my research company I manage a holiday property development

26

business. It's a family concern started by my father. My real interest is ecology though. Eventually I want to develop some eco friendly properties where people can spend a few days close to nature and learn all about the world we live in."

"But I don't know anything about you, or your companies," she protested. She wished her parents had passed on the 'try anything once' gene that had coloured her childhood. She knew her mother would already be packing by now, far too excited by the prospect of an adventure to worry about the disruption to her life. Claire, however, remembered the anxiety of being uprooted and sent to yet another school in another town only too well. Even after all this time her stomach still churned and she still felt sick when faced with a new situation. She stared at Daniel, panic building.

He pulled a couple of business cards from his pocket and handed them to her. Both had website addresses. Then he pushed back his chair and stood up.

"Look I know it's too much for you to take in right away, so how about I leave you to think about it. Check out the websites. One is for the family business and it will tell you everything you want to know about me. Call the company if you want to. Ask anything you like. You don't need to worry Carl will answer because he doesn't work there," he gave her an unapologetic grin.

"The other one is for my own research company. You'll be able to see what it's achieved so far and what the plans are for the future. That way you'll have your questions ready when I collect you from work at four o'clock. I'll drive you to your parent's house so we can discuss it on the way."

"But my parents live miles away," she protested, standing up as well.

"I know where they live Claire. You told me on Monday," he reminded her. "It's not a problem. What is a problem, however, is the fact that I have to be back in the States by Monday evening so we don't have much time to tie this up. Now are you going to eat your sandwiches or not?"

"Not," she said. She didn't know whether to be excited by his offer or to be angry at the way he was trying to organize her life.

"In that case I'll have them," he said, scooping them up. He bit into the first one as he made for the door.

Claire sat down again and remained at the table for another ten minutes, her coffee growing cold. She knew why Daniel Marchant thought she would be prepared to give up her life and her friends and travel to Florida, because she had already told him. She had said she was in a rut and needed a change at the same time she told him she didn't want a husband or even a date. As far as he was concerned she was a safe bet in a world where his family seemed to be trying to marry him off.

She would never be a threat to his self-imposed bachelorhood.

She drew in a long breath as she remembered his height and the width of his shoulders under his well-cut gray suit. Then she remembered his long, lean thigh muscles as he stretched his legs out under the table. She pulled on her coat with a sigh. If only he knew!

Chapter Three

True to his promise, Daniel was waiting for her outside the library when she left work at four o'clock. He was at the wheel of a black sedan that was parked half-on and half-off the sidewalk. Claire got in hurriedly as a traffic warden approached.

Daniel grinned at her, switching on the ignition as he did so. "Just in time! Which way now?"

"I need to go home to collect some clothes," she told him as she directed him down the nearest side street. "Then we need to beat the rush hour."

"Fine. I'll drop you off and go and find a gas station. Will twenty minutes be okay?

She nodded; relieved he didn't expect her to invite him into her apartment. Although she had learned quite a lot about him from a quick trawl of the company websites before she left work, she wasn't about to let her guard down. She had every intention of keeping her distance while she considered his job offer. However tempting it sounded, she would still tell him she needed the weekend to think about it.

* * *

Half an hour later they were aiming for the freeway. The traffic was too busy for serious conversation so they kept it to pleasantries while Daniel negotiated his way out of the city. Once on the open road, however, he filled her in on the details of the job he had in mind.

"The company has only been operating for a little over three years. At the moment we are concentrating on coastal habitats and the effect of climate change on migrating birds and marine life. Later on we're going to research terrestrial animals too. It's still a fairly small affair but thanks to a skeleton staff and lots of volunteers, it's beginning to influence coastal and wetlands conservation. It's doing good work, but slowly. I want to speed it up by employing someone who can catalogue the research and photograph some of the results. That's where you come in. With your experience you could set up some educational programs too."

Claire looked at him. It was dark now but she could see his profile, the way he was concentrating on the road ahead. He glanced across at her. Their eyes met for a fleeting moment before he returned his gaze to the rain-spattered windscreen. It was enough, though, for Claire's heart to start pumping double time.

She couldn't do this. She knew she was being ridiculous, knew she should grasp the opportunity he was offering her with both hands, but she couldn't do it. It was bad enough her stomach was already churning at the thought of moving somewhere new without the added complication of Daniel Marchant.

The memory of what it felt like to have her heart broken was still with her even though it was years since she'd been betrayed. When she was twenty she had fallen in love with an older man and started dreaming of the life they would have together. For a long time he had seemed to want the same thing, so when he left her for someone else she'd been utterly devastated. Unwilling to accept his rejection she'd made a fool of herself, pleading with him to give their relationship another chance. She had abandoned all pride; sure that he would soon realize his mistake. Nothing in her life had prepared her for the pain of having her heart thrown back in her face.

Five years on, although the hurt had gone, the memory of his betrayal still coloured her attitude to relationships. It was the main reason she was still footloose and fancy free because the experience had persuaded her it was better to stick to uncomplicated friendships. Until now she had only indulged in relationships that left her heart intact and her emotions untroubled.

This attitude had got her to the here and now without too many problems, but she knew Daniel Marchant was a different matter. Tall, tanned, and sun-bleached, he was the shadowy figure who roved through her barely acknowledged dreams. He even shared her interests. There was only one problem. He was so not interested in her except as an employee, that she could feel her heart breaking all over again as they drove along the dark ribbon of freeway.

"I'm sorry but…I don't…I can't do it," she said and her voice was unexpectedly shaky.

* * *

Despite Daniel's best efforts she hadn't changed her mind by the time he pulled into the overgrown driveway of her parent's house.

He could feel his frustration building. It had nothing to do with how he felt about her. It was prompted by her obstinate refusal to consider a job he was sure would fit her like a glove. Her librarian's training, combined with her skills as a photographer, were exactly what he needed. He was not offering her a sinecure just because he wanted to get to know her better; he was offering her a job that was made for her.

He hadn't been entirely sure of his intentions when he finally tracked her down to the city library. If anything he was hoping that a second meeting would prove to be disappointing, that she would turn out to be different in the clear light of day. He wanted his heart back before he made a fool of himself. He wanted to be able to return to Florida and concentrate on his plans without the complication of a tall, dark-haired woman with wide gray eyes and an infectious laugh. When he'd seen her working with a group of children, however, he'd been captivated all over again.

Unaware he was watching, she had talked to them with enthusiasm and humour. Then she had patiently answered their endless questions. When, at the end of the session, she had read them a story with feeling and flair, he had listened in fascination.

She was a natural communicator. She was someone who would empathize with everyone, from the very young to the very old, from the ignorant to those who thought they knew best. She had something few people had. She had an ability to connect, to use the right words, the right gestures, so everyone listening to her immediately wanted to know what would come next. He knew she would be an absolute godsend to his organisation. She would be able to help set up educational programmes and run workshops. She had the real skills necessary to adapt to the hundred and one things that everyone working for him had to do to keep it going.

He switched off the ignition and turned to her with a sigh. "I wish you'd change your mind," he said. "The job is made for you Claire. I'm sure you'd love it if you just gave it a chance."

* * *

Before she could answer the front door burst open and her mother appeared. She was wearing one of her usual flowing kaftans. With her gray hair braided around her head with a crimson scarf, she resembled an elegant exotic bird as she swooped towards the car.

"Darling, how lovely to see you!" she tugged the passenger door open and swept Claire into an extravagant embrace. For the briefest moment Claire clung to her, inhaling the familiar scent, feeling the softness of her wrinkled cheek. Then she gently pushed her away. She never allowed herself to get swept up by her mother's enthusiasm because she knew it would only last until something or someone else took her attention.

On cue, her mother noticed Daniel. "And who is this?" she demanded, immediately releasing Claire and walking round the car to the driver's door. She took in Daniel's six feet three inches with an appreciative gaze. Then she beckoned to Claire's father who had come to the door and was peering through the gloom.

"Arthur dear, come and say hello. Claire has brought a boyfriend home and a good looking one at that!"

"He's not my boyfriend Mum!" Claire protested hotly, but nobody was listening. Instead her parents were both greeting Daniel effusively. To her chagrin, he made no attempt to explain himself. Instead he returned their greeting enthusiastically with the trace of a wicked smile quirking the corner of his mouth.

* * *

Ten minutes later, with Claire's travel bag deposited in the hall, Claire and Daniel were each demolishing bowls of vegetable stew. Well Daniel was. Claire was toying with hers, pushing carrots and parsnips around in quiet desperation while her mother and father quizzed Daniel non-stop.

He took it in good part, although he only answered some of their questions. Claire noticed how skillfully he deflected them away from the areas of his life he deemed private. Nevertheless she learned a great deal more about him. She learned that as well as a brother he had three sisters, all younger than him. He also had a niece and a nephew. She learned, too, that both of his parents were alive but neither of them enjoyed good health.

"My father lost his sight a few years ago," he told them. "And the stress of caring for him has affected my mother so that these days she…she's no longer herself."

Claire heard a brief hesitation in his voice before he changed the subject so smoothly that nobody else seemed to notice. What did he mean, she wondered? Was his mother depressed? Despite herself, she was intrigued. Why didn't he want to talk about it? She watched him. He seemed totally relaxed as he scooped up the last of the stew and then smiled acceptance as her mother offered him some more.

"It's delicious," he told her. "As a dedicated carnivore I had no idea vegetables could be this good."

He had chosen exactly the right words to prompt her mother into a long lecture about the benefits of vegetarianism. As he listened he looked across at Claire. Seeing an inner turmoil shadowing his eyes she suddenly realized his compliment had been deliberate, a ploy to bring the inquisition to an end.

Suddenly she wanted to apologise for her parents' insensitivity. She was used to their never-ending stream of questions and she knew they were totally without guile. Despite having reached seventy, her mother and father remained two of life's innocents. Always willing to believe the best of people, they were too open themselves to understand how some people might prefer to keep their business private, and too inquisitive to consider restraint. She was still trying to find a way to draw their attention away from Daniel when her mother pre-empted her.

"Why don't you both go up to your room and freshen up while I make the coffee," she said.

A bubble of laughter instantly replaced the troubled expression in Daniel's eyes. He winked at Claire, and then leaving her to resolve the situation, pushed back his chair, stacked their dishes, and carried them to the sink.

Her sympathy for him forgotten, Claire scowled at his back view. He needn't think he was going to stay here. She had already spent too long with him for her own peace of mind. The last thing she wanted was to have him hanging around all weekend trying to persuade her to change her mind about his job.

"Daniel's not staying Mum. He has to leave soon because he has…he's busy tomorrow."

"What nonsense! Surely you don't expect the poor man to go back out into the night when he's already been driving for hours. He's tired, and anyway it's far too late. Besides, a storm is brewing. Set your old alarm clock when you go to bed. That way he can be up and off before the rest of us wake up if that's what he wants."

It's not just that…it's…we're not…that is we won't be sharing a bedroom," she said. She had already given up on any idea of persuading her parents they were not an item.

"Well you do surprise me dear! I had no idea you were so delightfully old-fashioned. It's not a problem though. I'll just go and find some more sheets and make up a bed for Daniel in the spare room."

By now Daniel was having a great deal of trouble keeping a straight face. Claire glared at him until her father left the table to go and fetch some fresh coffee from the cellar store. Then she exploded.

"That was totally uncalled for," she hissed. "You can see they take no notice of what I say, so the least you could have done was back me up. You could have explained to them that we only met last Monday. You could have told them you're here to offer me a job. Told them you've booked a hotel room."

"But I haven't," he said with an unrepentant grin. "Admittedly I was going to as soon as I dropped you off, but your parents are so welcoming, and so insistent that I stay, that it would be churlish to refuse."

"It would not!" she cried. And then, to her intense embarrassment, her eyes flooded with hot tears. Couldn't he see she didn't want him here? The last thing she wanted was to have to think of him asleep under the same roof with only the width of a wall between them.

He stopped grinning then and used his forefinger to wipe away the lone tear that trickled down her cheek. "Ah Claire, I'm sorry! I didn't mean to upset you. You're right of course. I shouldn't have teased you. I'll make my excuses and leave as soon as we've had coffee."

"You'll do no such thing," her father, returning from his trip to the cellar, heard the final part of Daniel's promise to Claire and misinterpreted it. "You won't disturb us if you have to leave early because we both sleep like babies. Besides, Sybil is right. A storm is blowing up so it's not the best time to be out on the road.

Against her better judgment, and because she knew she owed him for driving her home on what was a filthy night, Claire was forced to agree with him.

"He's right. It'll be better if you stay here, so why don't you go and fetch your bag."

Ignoring him, she concentrated on spooning coffee into the percolator. Then she assembled mugs, sugar and cream while Daniel propped himself on the corner of the table and watched her. Finally she let him off the hook. Checking that her father wasn't listening she met his questioning gaze full on.

"Go on. It'll be easier all round. They'll be upset if I fail to keep a man under their roof for one night. I'm already such a grave disappointment to them in that area that they have more or less given up on me."

He gave a doubtful nod as he left the kitchen. As soon as he was out of sight she dug into her pocket for a tissue. Then she scrubbed at the spot where his hand had touched her face, and blew her nose with unnecessary force.

* * *

While they drank their coffee Claire's parents talked about various local developments, including plans for a new supermarket. Knowing what their attitude was likely to be Claire asked them what they thought about it. It was a ploy to deflect their attention from Daniel, and she considering spending the rest of the evening listening to their plan to set up a village protest group a small price to pay. For the rest of the evening, although they dominated the conversation, they didn't ask a single question

40

about Claire's job, or about any other aspect of her life. She was used to it and didn't expect anything else, but she saw Daniel frown once or twice when they cut her off mid-flow because they had suddenly remembered something else they wanted to tell her.

"Don't you mind?" he asked when they eventually made their way upstairs.

She shook her head. "No. They've always been the same. It's not that they don't care about me. It's just that they find their own life and opinions infinitely more fascinating than mine. And if I'm honest, I don't blame them. They have led such an adventurous life that in their eyes I am merely existing from one pay packet to the next."

His fierce response surprised her. "Stop it Claire! Stop putting yourself down! Stop just putting up with life and begin to challenge it! Come to Florida. Do something different, something that will shake you out of the rut you say you're in."

"I can't!" she shook her head. "Just believe me. I can't."

"Yes you can, and if it takes me all weekend I'm going to persuade you. You need this job and my organisation needs you."

And I need you too, he added to himself as they said goodnight. It wasn't a comfortable thought but he couldn't avoid it. Why he wanted this contrary woman with her cloud of dark hair and her emotional hang-ups he couldn't imagine. Not when his increasingly frustrated family kept introducing him to a stream of available and uncomplicated beauties. Nor did he know whether he stood any sort of chance with her. He wasn't going to give up without a fight though. She might think she wasn't looking for a date but if he could only get her to Florida he would do everything in his power to change her mind.

Chapter Four

By the time Daniel appeared the following morning Claire had made a decision. Unable to think clearly during the long hours of the night because her overheated imagination kept picturing him in the adjoining room, she had tossed and turned until the darkness filtered to gray. Then she'd given up and gone down to the kitchen to make coffee and consider her options.

She could continue to take the coward's way out and turn her back on the job Daniel was offering her, or she could take a deep breath and plunge in heart first. Either choice would be painful.

She knew that turning down the opportunity to work in Florida would leave her regretful and disappointed for years to come. Accepting his invitation, however, would open up old scars of rejection and worthlessness as it became clearer and clearer that he wasn't interested in anything other than a working relationship with her. That Daniel would be unaware of her feelings was the only thing that made it remotely possible. After all, he couldn't throw her heart back at her if he didn't know he had it in the first place.

Her mother solved part of her dilemma. Usually a late riser, she surprised Claire by coming into the kitchen while she was still drinking her coffee. Dunking a teabag into a mug of hot water, she smiled knowingly at her daughter.

"Having trouble sleeping darling?"

"A bit," Claire admitted. Then she took in the full implication of her mother's sly glance and choked on a mouthful of coffee. Really it was too bad! Why couldn't she have a normal mother instead of one who immediately assumed that her early morning wakefulness was because she was frustrated?

Her mother forestalled her protest with a chuckle. "From the look of him I don't imagine that Daniel would be too upset if you did decide to knock on his bedroom door you know."

Claire glared at her in irritation. She was impossible! It was obvious she was totally convinced they were dating, and Claire knew from bitter experience that no amount of protest would change her mind. She decided not to waste her breath trying. Instead she made a decision.

"We'll be out all day," she said, determined to keep Daniel as far away from her parents as possible to avoid further embarrassment. "I'm going to show him the beach and the pinewoods, and then we'll probably drop into *The Lifeboat* for lunch."

Her mother nodded a relaxed acceptance of Claire's plan. She never minded how her visitors spent their time. It was one of the things Claire liked best about coming home. Although her parents had no interest in her life in the city, they didn't have expectations when she came home either, so she was free of obligation, free to do whatever she wanted, go wherever she wanted, or she had been until now. Unfortunately Daniel's presence seemed to be complicating things. It was obvious he intended to make the most of her parent's assumption that he and Claire were an item and stay for the entire weekend, so she had no choice but to entertain him.

Her mother drained her mug and started bustling around the kitchen, thinking aloud as she began to assemble the ingredients needed for a cooked breakfast. "I suppose you'd better have something hot before you set out...although I'll never understand what makes you want to go out and commune with nature in all weathers...and I think I'll make a nut roast for supper."

"You'll do no such thing," Daniel's deep drawl startled them both. "I'm going to take you all out for a meal this evening. It's the least I can do to repay your hospitality."

He stood in the doorway. He had addressing his remark to her mother but his eyes were on Claire. He had obviously heard her plans and was questioning her intention, hoping her decision to spend more time with him meant she was interested in the job.

He was dressed in jeans and a thick navy sweater. Still wet from the shower, his mussed up hair was the colour of warm treacle. She

45

ignored the effect his sudden appearance had on her pulse rate and forced a smile. "I hope you have some shoes suitable for walking because it'll be pretty rough underfoot after last night's storm."

"My hiking boots have achieved their own frequent flyer award," he told her with a relieved grin as he pulled his car keys from his pocket and made for the front door.

Claire's spirits lifted slightly when he returned carrying scuffed hiking boots in one hand and a thick weatherproof jacket in the other. If he came equipped for walking each time he travelled across the Atlantic, then he must be serious about wildlife. Maybe her decision to spend more time with him before she made up her mind about his job was the right one after all. A day fighting the elements would not only clear her head, it would show her exactly what Daniel Marchant was made of.

* * *

An hour later, protected from the wind by a thick padded jacket, and with her hair bundled into an old woollen hat, Claire led the way across the open heath. In the distance were the miles of undulating sand dunes that provided a wind and sea defence between the land and the beach. Daniel, similarly clad, followed her, a pair of powerful binoculars swinging from a leather strap around his neck.

They had barely exchanged half a dozen words since they left the house but somehow it didn't seem to matter. For the first time since their original meeting Claire felt at ease with him again. She could see from the expression on his face that he was as focussed as she was, his eyes alert for any sign of wildlife, his interest excited by the unusual terrain.

Over breakfast she had given him a potted history of the area. Now she was eager to show it to him.

The morning passed quickly as they trekked through pinewoods busy with red squirrels, and across uneven scrub where flocks of grazing birds rose in noisy protest as they disturbed them. Time and again Daniel raised his binoculars to his eyes with an exclamation of delight, and time and again Claire had to force her fast beating heart into submission as she responded to his enthusiasm and tried to answer his questions.

Eventually they moved shoreward, clambering across the sand dunes until they had an uninterrupted view of the sea. It was black and wild under scudding clouds that occasionally parted to reveal unexpected patches of pale blue sky. The beach below them, deserted except for an occasional dog walker, stretched for miles in both directions.

Daniel was silent for several long minutes as he slowly took in the panoramic view. Then he turned to Claire, his face full of barely repressed excitement.

"Look at those dunes! They go on forever. It's amazing!"

Claire stared at him, startled by his over-the-top enthusiasm for what, to her, was just a familiar hike, somewhere she enjoyed for its peace and its wild, windswept beauty.

When he saw the surprised expression on her face he chuckled. "You have absolutely no idea that this dunescape is one of the most important nature conservation areas in Europe, do you?" he teased. "To you it's just home, but I've read all about it, and to me it's a conservationist's dream. Don't worry though. I'll get over it. I tend to forget that most people aren't turned on by coastal erosion. Now how about lunch? I think you mentioned a local pub."

"Yes, *The Lifeboat Inn.* It's a fifteen minute walk from here if we approach it from the beach*,"* Claire pointed across the dunes to where a path meandered inland through misshapen pines that were pitted and bent by the constant buffeting of the wind.

"Good because I'm ravenous," Daniel ran down the dune at speed, jumping the final slope at the point where the spiky maram grass gave way to sand.

Claire followed more slowly as she pondered his enthusiasm. If only she affected him the same way. Instead, she now had to accept another reason for his insistence on driving her home last night. It hadn't just been about persuading her to take his job; it had been about visiting the rolling dunes of the northwest coast as well.

She watched him from her bird's eye view at the top of one of the tallest dunes. Out here, with the wind tugging at his clothes and a woollen hat pulled down over his ears, he seemed younger somehow, and carefree. He was certainly very different from the sophisticated businessman with jet lag who had shared a meal with her on Monday. He was different, too, from yesterday's pushy Daniel, the one who had tracked her down and dropped such a bombshell of a job offer into her life, and then had managed to invade her home as well as her heart.

It was obvious he knew a great deal about conservation too. His knowledge about the local area proved it, as had his questions during their hike. Time and time again she had found herself responding eagerly to his enthusiasm, anxious to share her own knowledge with him, so why was she holding back about the job?

You're just a coward Claire Harris, she told herself as she negotiated the downward slope. *You're not prepared to take risks with anything, especially your heart, so serve you right if you do end up an old maid, just like Jenny said you would.*

"Ow…Ow…Ouch!" All further thoughts were forgotten as the edge of the sand dune gave way beneath her and toppled her all the way down to the beach. She landed with a thump and before she could catch her breath another section of the dune sheared away, covering her in sand and leaving layers of soil and roots exposed to the elements. Strong arms pulled her free and then supported her as she struggled to her feet.

"Don't do that!" Daniel seized both her hands in one of his as she tried to brush soil and sand from her face and clothes. Then he made a systematic search of his pockets with the other.

Claire was too surprised to resist. Instead she peered blurrily at him as her tear ducts attempted to wash the sand and grit away. He didn't release his grip and she heard concern in his voice when he spoke to her.

"You seem to have cut yourself or something."

Finally he found a tissue in one of his pockets, wadded it into a pad, and pressed it against the side of her face. When he took it away it was scarlet with blood.

Claire gritted her teeth against a wave of sudden nausea and tried to ignore the small army of black dots that were beginning to cloud her vision. She wasn't going to do this! She wasn't going to faint in front of Daniel Marchant so that he could add *faints at the sight of blood* to the list of fears and ignorance he seemed to be uncovering.

She couldn't fool him though. He saw the colour drain from her face and felt her wobble as her knees began to give way. Cursing under his breath he locked his arms around her and gently lowered her onto the sand.

"Don't do this to me Claire! Don't faint! Come on! Look at me! It's not as bad as all that. It just needs cleaning up. You must have knocked it against a tree root or something when you fell. You'll be fine once it's clean."

She shook her head weakly. "It's not that…it's the blood…I…ouch!"

The black dots were swiftly replaced by a feeling of extreme discomfort as he pushed her head down over her chest and held it there.

"Sorry about this but it's the only way I know to stop someone from fainting," he told her.

Her indignation was muffled as she spoke into the woolly scarf looped round her neck. "Well it certainly works! I'm fine now, or I would be if I could breathe!"

The pressure behind her neck eased allowing her to life her head and glare at him. "There was no need for the strong arm treatment. I wouldn't have fainted."

"So you say," he looked unconvinced as he dabbed at her cheek again. "It's not bleeding quite as much now but you need to get it cleaned and covered. Do you think you can make it to the inn you mentioned?"

"To *The Lifeboat?* Yes, of course I can," Claire began to get to her feet but Daniel was there before her.

"Whoa! Not so fast! Get up slowly and lean on me."

He kept his arms around her, leaving her no choice but to do as he said. He didn't take them

51

away once she was upright either. Instead, he merely settled one hand firmly on her waist and tilted her face towards him with the other one so that he could get a clearer look at her injury. Instinctively she jerked her head away. He was far too close for comfort. She could feel the warmth of his breath on her cheek. She could see how the Florida sun had bleached the curling tips of his eyelashes, and there was a tiny mole at the side of his mouth that she hadn't noticed before, and a…

Daniel stopped inspecting the cut on her cheek and looked at her. "Are you OK? Did I hurt you or something?"

"No. I'm fine," she said. "I'm just a bit woozy, that's all."

He looked at her doubtfully. "Well lean on me then and tell me the minute you feel shaky."

* * *

The journey to the inn seemed to take forever. Claire felt she was wading through treacle as she put one leg in front of the other, but the feeling had nothing to do with the cut on her face and everything to do with Daniel's proximity. She couldn't escape the arm holding her close to his side, nor the way the warmth of his body seemed to burn through her jacket, sending sparks of desire deep into the pit of her stomach.

She forgot about her injury as she wrestled with her reactions. This was ridiculous! He was someone she had only just met, someone who wasn't remotely interested in settling down, someone who had made it clear that he wasn't even looking for a girlfriend, so why had she decided to fall for him, or at least why had her treacherous body decided to fall for him? It couldn't be anything more than his good looks because she still wasn't sure who Daniel was.

Was he the serious businessman she had first met, or the pushy stranger who had tracked her down and, seemingly without effort, taken over her life, or was he the carefree Daniel who was so enthusiastic about the sandy, windswept countryside surrounding her parent's home.

"You're very quiet. Are you sure you're okay?" He broke into her thoughts, slowing both of them down so he could look at her again.

"I'm fine," she lied, slanting her gray gaze upwards. For one long moment they stood looking at one another, then Daniel's unencumbered arm moved up towards her face. His long golden brown eyes widened slightly as she sucked in a breath and caught her bottom lip between her teeth. As he dipped his head towards her, her lips parted for the kiss that never came. Instead he tugged her hat down onto her head, wrapped her scarf more tightly around her neck, and started moving forward again, matching his stride to hers.

"Come on. You can't afford to get chilled, not when you've had such a shock. The sooner we reach *The Lifeboat* the better."

The last thing Claire was likely to be was chilled. She felt red hot, partly with need, but mainly with embarrassment. Had Daniel seen how much she had wanted him to kiss her? If he had then he couldn't have given her a clearer message. His actions spoke for themselves. He had no interest in her other than as a possible work colleague and as someone who, right at this moment, he had to take care of, so the sooner she got that into her thick skull the better.

Chapter Five

Daniel didn't relax until Claire reappeared. She had washed away the dirt and sand and seemed fine despite a large square plaster on the side of her face.

Worried that the sight of congealed blood would make her feel faint again, he had refused to let her deal with her injury alone and had kept her close to his side until the barmaid was free to help. She had taken one look at Claire's face and produced a first aid kit from beneath the bar.

"Don't worry. Sit there and enjoy your drink. She'll be as good as new in no time." She had given him a cheerful smile as she took Claire's arm and led her to the women's bathroom.

He had ordered a pint of beer and swallowed half of it in one go, not because he was thirsty but because he needed something to settle his jangled nerves.

It had been a close escape but at least he had managed not to kiss her, not even when her face had been so close to his he could feel her breath on his cheek and see the black circles that rimmed the clear gray of her irises. Mesmerised, he had dipped his head towards her, unable to help himself, but then he had heard her quick intake of breath, felt the recoil as she stiffened in his arms, and had had the sense to start walking again.

Whatever had he been thinking of? He had almost blown everything. He needed to stay focused on the fact that she didn't want a relationship with anyone. After all she had told him so when they first met and nothing in her behaviour since then indicated she had changed her mind, or that she was in anyway interested in him. Just the opposite in fact! She had also told him, fairly forcefully, that she didn't want to work in Florida, although something about the way she had said it had left a tiny seed of hope. And it was that hope which was keeping him here, ungallantly ignoring the fact that she didn't really want him in her parent's house.

Now, as she approached him, solemn faced, he felt a twinge of trepidation. Had she noticed how much he had wanted to kiss her? He hoped not. He didn't want to think about it, and he especially didn't want to think about what her reaction would have been if he had succeeded. She might put herself down, fade into the background when she was with her parents, but he was under no illusion that she was a pushover. She was entirely her own person. Strong-minded, determined, and very decidedly someone who would do the choosing as far as being kissed was concerned.

He gave her a half smile. She smiled back. And then they were laughing about her ungainly fall, her silly reaction to the sight of her own blood, the fact she had unknowingly taken him to one of the best nature conservancy areas in the country, and it was fine. It was a repeat of that first meeting when, after a rocky start, they had had a thoroughly enjoyable evening. This felt the same and they continued to talk well into the afternoon, long after the soup and sandwiches they had ordered had been cleared away and they were the only two people left in the bar. They would have sat there for longer if Claire hadn't glanced out of the window and noticed that the clear northern light was beginning to fade.

"It's time we made tracks before it's too dark to see where we're going. That is, unless you want to walk home through the village and admire the street lamps."

He grinned at her. "You know I don't want to do that, but what about you? Are you up to walking back across country?"

She snorted indignantly. "I only scratched my face. My legs and arms are still functioning perfectly well."

"Not wobbly then?"

She gave him a haughty look as she gathered up her coat and scarf in preparation for a renewed onslaught from the wind, but as she wrapped herself up he saw a smile shadow the corners of her mouth.

* * *

Their return journey was brisk. No stopping this time to watch the wildlife or look at the scenery. Not that they needed to stop for the view. It was all around them as they walked towards the setting sun for, in the capricious way of English weather, most of the clouds had cleared during the afternoon leaving a pale sky that was now streaked orange with red and purple highlights. It provided a dramatic backdrop to the flocks of geese returning from a day out at sea, and to the rooks shrieking and arguing above the treetops.

For most of the journey Daniel and Claire were silent. They had talked themselves out during lunch and now, with the plummeting temperature promising an overnight frost, they walked fast, anxious to escape the biting wind.

Claire glanced surreptitiously at Daniel as he strode along beside her. Her plan to survive the weekend in his company by walking him to a standstill while remaining cool and distant had backfired badly. He'd not only out-walked her, he'd taken care of her when she hurt herself, teased her out of her reserve, and then turned the whole day into one she would cherish for a long time. If he had only shown in the smallest way he found her as attractive as she found him then, despite her earlier misgivings, she might have been tempted to take her chances and reconsider his job offer. He hadn't though. Not once. Not even when she fell and hurt herself. Oh he had picked her up, shown real concern, and taken care of her and her wounds, but he had done all of it without showing a flicker of desire. Not even during that breathless moment when she had foolishly thought he *was* going to kiss her when, instead, all he had wanted to do was check her injury and straighten her hat. No! Her first decision was the right one. At the end of the weekend she would say goodbye to him and forget about working in Florida. That way she wouldn't get her heart broken all over again.

It wasn't until her parent's ramshackle old house came into view that she had another thought, one that momentarily stopped her in her tracks. Daniel hadn't once mentioned the job he was offering her, even though they had been together for most of the day. He hadn't talked about himself either. Instead he had talked about anything and everything else. He had enthused about the undulating countryside and the wild seascape around them and compared it to what he was used to in Florida. He had teased her about her ignorance of the local conservation area. He had asked her more questions about her peripatetic childhood and her life in the city, but all without giving anything personal away except for the most superficial information. Despite spending hours in his company she still knew hardly anything about his life on the other side of the Atlantic Ocean. He seemed to have forgotten about the job offer too.

Her eyes darkened with unexpected pain. She scowled and asked herself what else did she expect? It was entirely her own fault. She couldn't have it both ways. She had told him several times, and very forcibly, that she wasn't interested in his job, so she had no cause to complain if he took her at her word and prepared to move on. After all, he had made it abundantly clear he only saw her as a prospective colleague, and there must be plenty of other people out there with the right skills and qualifications who would fit the bill.

Realizing that she was no longer with him, Daniel stopped and turned around to look for her. She was standing stock still a few paces behind him. Her nose and cheeks were red from the cold and the wind, the white plaster was stark against her cheek, there were slight shadows under her huge gray eyes, and a curl of her blue-black tumbling hair had escaped from under her hat. She looked dishevelled and tired…and totally and utterly desirable. As he watched her, his breath caught in his throat. She saw him waiting and, giving him a wan smile, began to move forward again.

"Are you OK?" he asked, wondering how much longer he could keep up the pretence that he had no interest in her other than as a casual friend and a prospective employee. "Do you need to lean on me again?"

She stuffed her hands into her pockets and gave a resolute shake of her head. "I'm fine. All I need is a warm drink and a hot bath and I'll be as good as new."

* * *

Much later, cocooned in the cheerful, noisy warmth of a local restaurant, Claire sipped her wine and let her mind wander as her mother held court. She had seen and heard it all before. Charmed by Daniel's impeccable manners, and exhilarated by the surroundings, she was retelling stories of her own bohemian childhood and enchanting him with glimpses of the life she had lived before Claire was born. And it was interesting if you were a stranger like Daniel, not least because both her parents were born storytellers; always ready to perform to a willing audience.

She watched him as he smiled and nodded and asked questions in all the right places. It was just like that first evening when, against her better judgement, he had persuaded her that she would be doing him a favour if she ate with him. Only this time he was charming her parents instead. He couldn't help it. The courtesy, the charm, the warm interest came to him as naturally as breathing. He liked people. He was interested in their lives. It was how he was. She had to accept that the meal that she had so enjoyed last Monday, the interest he had shown in her, had been nothing to do with her personally at all. Despite his jet lag, he had swallowed his irritation and invited her to eat with him as a way of apologising for his brother's cross behaviour, not because he had been attracted to her. And it was the same now. This evening was all about thanking her parents for welcoming him into their home.

Another dream bites the dust she told herself with a wry smile at the waiter as he placed a large bowl of pasta in front of her. *I'd better not tell Jenny about this one though. If she ever gets to know I turned down Florida I'll never hear the last of it.*

Daniel's voice cut across her thoughts and brought her back to the here and now. "Are you okay Claire? You seem to be miles away."

"Claire spends most of her life day-dreaming," her mother answered for her. "She isn't interested in the fact that there's a great big world out there. She would rather spend her days in a library reading books instead of living a life." She gave a sharp little laugh as she shook back her hair. It made the rows of beads around her neck and the golden hoops dangling from her ears sparkle in the candlelight.

"I think you're mistaken," surprisingly Daniel's voice took on a slightly steely tone as his eyes locked with Claire's. "Claire is very much interested in the world. In fact she's considering coming to Florida to take up a job I've offered her."

Claire's mother responded with a peal of laughter that was loud enough to attract the attention of the diners at the next table. "If you truly believe that Daniel, then she's been leading you on. Claire won't go anywhere. When she was a child she was very obstinate about trying anything new, and she's the same now. She used to have tantrums whenever we wanted to move on. She even asked if she could be a boarder so she wouldn't have to keep changing schools, but we told her not to be so silly. We said it was much better to experience new things and make new friends instead of living a life surrounded by rules and regulations."

Suddenly Claire had had enough of being the target of her mother's amusement even though she knew everything she said was true. She *had* been a shy and difficult child. She *had* hated moving on and having to make new friends, but she'd done it and, if she was being totally honest with herself, it had taught her some useful lessons. For example she had learned to summon up a cool and confident air that fooled all but the most discerning however churned up she might be inside. She did it now. Eyes flashing she turned to her mother.

"That was years ago, Mum. I'm an adult now and it would be nice if you sometimes gave me credit for it. And, surprised as you might be to hear it, I *have* decided to take up Daniel's job offer. I'll be going to Florida as soon as I've worked out my notice at the library."

After a stunned silence her parents' reaction was everything she could have wished for. Her father sat and beamed at her and her mother swiftly jettisoned her slightly disparaging air. In its place was genuine enthusiasm and interest, and soon they were all talking about Daniel's company and how Claire fitted into it. They even toasted her success with the last of the red wine, and made plans to store her belongings while she was away.

Claire smiled and nodded and agreed with everything everybody said as she tried to persuade herself the fleeting look of triumph she had seen on Daniel's face when she had made her announcement had been a figment of her imagination. It had been gone in a moment, replaced by a warm smile of approval and questions about timing and how long it would be before she was free to travel. It had been enough, though, for Claire to realize he had manipulated her into doing exactly what he wanted. So much for her thinking he had given up on her. He'd just waited until he found a way to make her agree, and her mother had handed him one on a plate.

She sighed as he signalled for the bill. Why had she fallen for it? Why had she allowed her pride to direct her tongue and agree to something she knew would break her heart? She bent down to pick up her wrap but Daniel was there before her. He tucked it across her shoulders and handed her her purse.

"I'm glad you've changed your mind," was all he said, but his proximity, the warmth of his body, the spicy tang of his aftershave as he stood close to her, made her regret her impetuosity all over again. How was she going to bear it?

Chapter Six

The same feeling of trepidation washed over her again when, six weeks later, she pushed a laden luggage trolley out onto the arrivals concourse and saw Daniel waiting for her. All the way across the Atlantic she had told herself things would have changed, that he would no longer have the power to send her pulse rate into overdrive, that his attraction had been a thing of the moment, an aberration. One look was all it took to blow her theory to smithereens. She tightened her grip on the trolley and pasted a smile on lips that were suddenly dry as she walked towards him.

"Claire!" his deep voice was full of welcome as he greeted her. "How was the flight? Not too tiring I hope."

"It was fine. Thank you for the ticket. I wasn't expecting to travel Business Class."

He waved away her thanks as he took charge of the trolley and led the way to the exit. Claire followed, unable to stop feasting her eyes on the muscular planes of his back under a cotton T, and the lazy stride of his long, denim-clad legs. What was she doing here, courting heartbreak, when she could have stayed safely at home? One letter telling Daniel that, on reflection, she had decided to decline his offer, was all it would have taken. One letter, and a few days of regret, and it would have been over, whereas now she had to see it through. Had to stay for the six months she had promised. Had to honour the contract she had signed.

She sighed. Thank goodness she had at least insisted on a trial period, although, right at this moment, with Daniel's smile of welcome still burning into her brain, six months seemed like an eternity.

The problem was she hadn't been able to talk to anyone about how she felt because everyone she knew had been so thrilled for her. Her parents, because they thought that at long last she was showing some of their adventurous spirit; her colleagues, who were all envious of the sudden excitement that had invaded the library; and Jenny, who was quite sure there was a lot more to Daniel's job offer than Claire was prepared to admit, and who hadn't stopped quizzing her until she actually boarded the plane and turned off her cell phone. And all of this collective enthusiasm had boxed Claire into a corner, forcing her to bury her misgivings and accept their congratulations and advice while she worked out her notice and organized her departure.

Her new work colleagues hadn't helped either because as soon as Daniel had returned to Florida they had begun to make contact, acting as if she were already part of the team, their cheerful enthusiasm scuppering any lingering idea she might have had about backing out of the whole deal.

First it had been Scott, the Operations Manager.

"Was I glad when Daniel told me about you," he said. Then he offered to send her some reading material so she wouldn't be a complete novice when she arrived.

"You sound like exactly the person I need to help me keep my head above water. Of course you'll have to be prepared to work twenty-four-seven and then some, but I don't suppose Daniel mentioned that!"

Claire had laughed with him and then read everything he sent her several times over. And the very act of getting involved had helped to contain her nervousness about changing her job. By the time she had absorbed all the information that kept pinging into her email inbox, she was beginning to look forward to working with Scott, and her excitement about the prospect of doing something that would make a real difference was beginning to overshadow her nervousness.

Then Beth had called her.

"On the books it says I'm Corporate Secretary," she told Claire by way of an introduction. "But in actual fact I'm just the general dogsbody around here. I get all the jobs nobody else has time for, like finding you somewhere to live!"

Claire, who was still trying, without much success, to come to terms with everything that was happening to her, hadn't given such practicalities a thought. Beth's phone call jolted her into a sudden realisation of how soon her life was about to change.

"I…that's very kind of you," she said and then stopped, unsure what was expected of her.

Beth chuckled at the other end of the phone line. "I can tell from your voice you haven't even thought about it yet, have you?" she challenged. When Claire admitted she hadn't, she offered some options.

"I can book you into a hotel for a week or so while you have a look around for yourself, or you can trust me to find something for you."

"But surely finding me somewhere is an awful lot of work for you?" Claire protested.

"It really isn't. Don't forget the family business is all about holiday properties, so we're awash with apartments down here. If it's okay with you I'll find something I would be prepared to live in and stock it up with the basics."

"That is so kind of you," Claire found herself rapidly warming to the woman on the other end of the telephone. Her voice was so welcoming that she sounded as if she might become a friend, someone who could help take her mind off Daniel by introducing her to other people.

"Nonsense! I'll enjoy it. As soon as you return your signed copy of the contract I'll start looking. I'll also book you a plane ticket as soon as you let me know the actual date you can travel."

After that the rest of their conversation revolved around the upheaval involved in moving continents, although Beth had also asked her a few personal questions.

"It's just so I can get some idea of what sort of place you would like to live in," she explained as she prepared to end the call. "Daniel was next to useless when I asked him. For all I know you could be a penthouse suite sort of girl!

Then they had laughed together as Claire assured her that she most certainly was not, and a two-room apartment would be fine. Beneath the banter, however, she had experienced a fleeting sense of disappointment. Not only had Daniel not telephoned her since returning to the States, he hadn't even bothered to tell Beth anything about her. And he could have done. After all he had learned plenty on that fateful weekend, the weekend when he had out-maneuvered her, the weekend when her stupid pride had ignored her heart.

Briefly she wondered if Beth knew how they had met, then she shrugged the thought away. Of course not! If her experience was anything to go by, then Daniel Marchant was exceedingly tight lipped about all things personal. To Beth she would be just another employee, someone he had come across on his travels who just happened to have the qualifications needed in his organisation.

* * *

Shaking off the memory of her conversation with Beth, Claire lengthened her stride to match Daniel's, determined to start behaving like a grownup instead of a moonstruck teenager.

"Scott and Beth have been so helpful," she told him as they negotiated the car park. "I can't wait to meet them."

"The feeling appears to be mutual," he said, glancing across at her, his eyes full of rueful humour. "So much so that Beth seems to have put the day-to-day work on hold while she concentrates on organizing your apartment, and Scott has moved the filing cabinet into the entrance hall and shifted everything around in the office to make room for your desk."

Claire's face flushed with pleasure, even though she protested she hadn't meant to cause so much disruption. It was good to know that, despite her misgivings about working with Daniel, other people were looking out for her, and looking forward to meeting her.

* * *

The journey to her new home took much longer than Claire had anticipated, so when Daniel pulled into a rest area and suggested they stop for something to eat she was only too happy to comply.

"I didn't realize how hungry I was," she told him as she tucked into a plate of sizzling paprika chicken garnished with peppers and onion.

He smiled at her. "I make the same journey too often not to know when it's time to eat," he said. "I learned long ago the best way to deal with time change is to eat local time from the moment the plane hits the runway."

Claire laughed. "I seem to remember it's how we first met."

"So it was," his smile grew wider as he recollected their first meeting. "I was about to grab something to eat when Carl's voicemail came through telling me he had set up a date. Irritated as I was at the time, it did at least mean that I ended up finding you, so, on behalf of my company, thanks Carl!"

They both laughed as he clinked his ice-cold glass of water against hers.

"What did you say to him when you got home?" Claire was curious.

"Only that I'd prefer him to concentrate on his own life in future and keep out of mine."

"He'll still know it's me though, won't he? After all he set up our so called date, so he's bound to recognize my name if we ever meet."

Daniel shook his head. "Don't worry about it. You'll certainly meet him. It's not possible to avoid anyone in a place as small as Dolphin Key, but I can guarantee he won't mention it."

"You sound very sure of that."

"Oh I am!" Daniel chuckled as he remembered his conversation with his brother. "Carl isn't likely to mess with me again for a long time, not if he knows what's good for him."

He saw Claire's eyes widen and the chuckle turned into an easy laugh. "I forgot. You don't have brothers or sisters do you? It's okay! I didn't threaten him or anything. We just came to a brotherly agreement that he would live his life and I would live mine. I also told him if he ever breathed a word of what he'd done then I would dredge up a few childhood memories to share with Beth!"

"Beth?" Now Claire was thoroughly puzzled.

"Yes Beth. Didn't she tell you she's married to him?"

* * *

By the time they pulled up outside the apartment Claire was going to live in for the next six months, she was dizzy with tiredness. She had forced herself to stay awake for most of the journey, only nodding off for a few minutes at a time as Daniel's dark blue Range Rover ate up the miles.

"Careful of your ankles, there are rocks here and lose stones," Daniel steadied her as she stepped down from the car into a blackness that was so dense she couldn't see the ground. "Stay

72

right where you are while I fetch the flashlight from the trunk."

"Is it…um…always this dark?" Claire, who was used to a streetlight shining outside her bedroom window back in the city, tried to penetrate the darkness without success.

"No, but the moon doesn't seem to want to play ball tonight," Daniel's disembodied voice was deadpan. He relented when he switched on the flashlight and shone its beam away from the car towards the black outline of a building standing foursquare in front of them.

"Don't worry. Although you can't see them from here, there are safety lights along the walkway at ground level. If you'd rather stay somewhere where there are streetlights, though, then tell Beth. She'll be happy to find you a different apartment."

"No! It's fine. I guess I just wasn't expecting it to be so dark," Claire swung her flight bag onto her shoulder and retrieved her jacket from inside the car. She had no intention of letting Daniel add *afraid of the dark* to the list of hang-ups he had already uncovered. And what could be so bad about it anyway? After all she was going to be living in an apartment block with other people, so if something scared her in the middle of the night then she would be able to share it with someone. Making a firm resolution to get to know her nearest neighbours as quickly as possible, she slammed the car door shut and gingerly felt her way around to where Daniel was lifting her suitcases out of the trunk.

He handed her the flashlight. "You look after this while I take care of your luggage."

Feeling better now she had charge of illuminations, Claire shone the beam ahead of them as they picked their way across an area of rough ground dotted with hillocks of coarse grass, rocks ready to trip the unwary, and an area of shingle. Then they were on a boardwalk that led, finally, to a covered walkway and an elevator.

* * *

Daniel, following on behind, took in every detail of Claire's silhouette; the long, denim encased legs, the square determination of her shoulders, the tangle of upswept hair revealing the slender stem of her neck, and felt himself being sucked into a future where he had no control.

Unlike Claire, he hadn't expected their time apart to diminish her attraction, nor had he had any second thoughts about enticing her to Florida. From the moment he first met her he knew how he felt about her and he wasn't expecting that to change anytime soon. So, with characteristic single-mindedness, he had done something about it, and then buried himself in his work. It had left him with little time to think and even less time to worry about what would happen when she arrived, so when he had set off for the airport he hadn't considered how he might react when he saw her again.

Tall and striking in black denims and a scarlet jacket, she had been easy to spot, and he had already raised his hand to wave to her when their eyes met. She hadn't smiled. She had just acknowledged him with a cool gray gaze as she walked towards him, her expression unreadable.

He had greeted her cheerfully, made small talk, taken charge of her luggage, all without touching her, when what he had actually wanted to do was sweep her into his arms and kiss her for a long, long time. The interminable journey to Dolphin Key and the stop off to eat hadn't helped either. Having Claire so tantalizingly close and yet not be able to touch her had taken far more will power on his part than he would have thought possible.

Now, under cover of the darkness that surrounded them, he let his guard down for the short time it took them to reach the elevator, and recalled the moment when, glancing across at Claire, he saw she had fallen asleep, her head resting sideways against the window. Free to look at her without worrying she might think he was coming-on to her; he had divided his gaze between the dark ribbon of the freeway and her sleeping profile for several uninterrupted minutes. Although it had been too dark for him to see her in detail, every shadow and curve of her face had etched itself into his brain, and it had been the moment he realized that for him it really was Claire or nobody.

Offering her a job, persuading her to move to Florida, had been part of a half-formed plan, a way of getting to know her better under the camouflage of working together. Behind it came the hope that, given time and familiarity, she would begin to reciprocate his feelings and rethink her views on dating. Now, however, with her sitting beside him as his car ate away the miles, he knew he had taken an irrevocable step, and if he couldn't make her want him then he would be heart sore for a very long time.

He didn't have the first clue why he felt this way. Nor did he like it. It undermined his faith in who he was. The Daniel Marchant who had forsworn all serious relationships so he could concentrate on the two jobs he was trying to hold down whilst also building his vision of the future, was no more. Instead he was a mess of conflicting emotions that all centred on the girl at his side and which, if he gave them the upper hand, might scupper all his plans.

What if he couldn't persuade her to stay for longer than her six-month contract? What if he never managed to persuade her he was the right person for her? What if he never got past first base on her emotional chart? What if he *did* persuade her but she wanted to return to her home in England? What if…

The arrival of the elevator brought him back to the here and now. As they squeezed in with the suitcases, he forced a smile. "It's not usually so crowded but not many of the people staying here bring six month's worth of clothes."

"I've probably packed far too much but Beth said to come prepared for most eventualities," Claire gave him an answering smile across the pile of luggage.

"Please don't tell me you've brought a snow suit," Daniel aimed for light banter, anything to keep things uncomplicated between them. He could still remember the vehemence with which Claire had declared she wasn't looking for a husband, partner, or even a boyfriend, so this was certainly not the time for him to make any sort of move. The last thing he wanted was for her to think he had brought her over so he could hit on her. No! He was going to have to keep his feelings strictly under control for the foreseeable future.

Chapter Seven

Claire stood in the centre of the large open plan room and turned in a slow circle. Now Daniel had gone she could concentrate, take in the surroundings that were going to be her home for the next six months.

The apartment was on the top floor of what appeared to be a large, wooden building, although it was difficult to tell in the darkness. She could hear the sound of the sea too, not loud, but loud enough to indicate it was nearby. Tomorrow was soon enough to explore though. It was far too dark to even bother to pull aside the drapes and go out onto the balcony that Daniel said ran the length of the apartment. Instead, she studied the interior and approved of the simple white paintwork, the blue upholstery, the rush matting on varnished floorboards, the blond wood of the kitchenette and, bliss upon bliss, the huge bowl of fresh oranges sitting on the kitchen counter beside a state-of-the-art juicer.

Too tired to even pull a bottle of water from the refrigerator, she turned towards the bathroom. Unpacking would have to wait until tomorrow. She didn't even bother to go in search of her toothbrush. Instead she used the one that was in the complementary travel bag an air attendant had handed to her, and which she had stashed in her carry-on before she left the aircraft.

Then, after making sure that the door was secure, she made her way up a tightly spiraling staircase to a tiny bedroom in the eaves. Also furnished in white and blue but with the addition of citrus yellow flowers on the counterpane, it was fresh and airy. Throwing off her clothes, she opened a window. Mosquito netting was fixed across it and it was the unfamiliarity of the net, more than anything else, that made her realise how far away from home she was, and from everything familiar.

* * *

As Claire rolled over in bed she tried to identify the noise that had woken her. It sounded like a particularly tetchy baby and for a moment she wondered if one of her near neighbours was pacing the floor with a crying infant. Then, as full consciousness kicked in, she realized it was the raucous shout of a seagull and it was so close it might as well have been in the bedroom with her.

Suddenly wide awake and keen to explore her surroundings, she threw back the bedcovers, pulled on the T-shirt she had worn on her flight over, and made her way, barefoot, down the twisty stairs. Ten minutes later, having got to grips with the juicer, she dragged back the heavy blue drapes, fumbled with the door catch, and then stepped out onto the balcony with a glass of fresh orange juice in her hand. She didn't lift it to her lips, however. Instead, she abandoned it onto a small metal table that stood to one side of the balcony next to a stack of collapsible chairs, and took the two steps necessary to reach the railing. With her hands resting on the smooth, weathered wood, she stared out onto an expanse of water that exactly reflected the first pink streaks of dawn painting the sky. Overhead the seagull scolded her for disturbing its early morning solo.

A sound halfway between a sigh and a sob escaped her as she gazed in amazement at her surroundings. In front of her the view slowly coalesced into something picture postcard perfect as the pinks softened to apricot, to yellow, and then to a clear, soft daylight as the sun finally breached the horizon and settled into its morning routine.

Nobody had told her she would be living on a beach curving around a bay of water that was so calm its ripples barely frilled the white sand at its edge; a beach with views out to small islands lush with vegetation; a beach protected on one side by a small rock strewn promontory, and on the other by the ramshackle order of a small fishing pier that was already showing signs of early morning activity.

She watched as a lone fisherman busied himself with lines and bait, while someone else who was dressed in a green fleece and a black baseball cap tied an inflatable dinghy to one of the supporting pillars. Suddenly she wanted to be there too. She wanted to see Dolphin Key and her new home from a different perspective. She wanted to know what the fisherman hoped to catch. She wanted to get up close to the cluster of pelicans squabbling over a mess of spilt bait.

Reclaiming her orange juice she gulped it down, left the empty glass on the table, and took the stairs to her bedroom two at a time. In moments she had pulled on her jeans, passed a cursory brush through her hair, unearthed a cotton sweater and a pair of trainers from the bottom of one of her suitcases, and was ready to go. For a moment her hands hovered above her camera but then she turned away. Now was not the time. She needed to get a feel for the place first, learn all about it. There would be plenty of time for photos later.

* * *

The beach was deserted except for several sandpipers bobbing about at the tide line. Claire watched them for a moment before she scattered them by walking across the white sand to investigate the clumps of seaweed and shingle that had been washed in by the tide.

Twenty minutes later, having trawled every inch of the tiny beach, and poked at every piece of flotsam, she climbed up onto the road and made her way across to the pier. It was busier now. A truck, with a trailer attached, was unloading a motorboat onto the slipway, and a few more fishermen had arrived and were standing in a group. Without pausing in their discussion, they nodded as she walked past them. Claire gave a shy smile. She wasn't used to being acknowledged by complete strangers because in recent years she had chosen to be a city girl, not someone living somewhere as small as Dolphin Key.

Less than a thousand inhabitants, Daniel had told her when he was filling in the details about the job. What else had he said? That its main income came from tourism; that it took ecology seriously; that it was an ideal place to get away from the pressures of life. And something else too! She paused in her stroll along the pier. Something about everybody knowing everybody else's business. Something about it not just being the summer heat that was stifling. Then he had laughed and changed the subject, telling her to take no notice of him; saying it would be different for her because she hadn't been brought up there.

She leaned on the railing and stared across the bay to her new home, keen to see it from a new perspective. She noticed she had left the door to the balcony wide open and quickly dismissed it. At four stories up her apartment was hardly going to be a major attraction for any would be intruder. With a shrug she turned her attention to the building as a whole and immediately her face creased into a delighted smile. She was living in a wooden clapboard house, ON STILTS, for goodness sake! She guessed it was to protect it from flooding but it still felt as if she was living in a storybook...apart from the bit about being rescued by a handsome prince of course, because unfortunately her particular handsome prince had made it very clear he had other far more important things to occupy him. She sighed. Whatever had got into her? This was the twenty-first century, and damsels, distressed or otherwise, had been looking out for themselves for a very long time.

* * *

"Good morning. Did you sleep well?" The voice and the question came from somewhere beneath her line of vision.

Peering over the railing she saw Daniel smiling up at her from the stern of the dinghy she had noticed from her balcony. He was the man in the baseball cap, except that now he had taken it off and tossed it into the bottom of the boat where it perched on a coil of ropes, next to several nets and a small rucksack.

It took her a moment to push the fact she had been thinking of him to the back of her mind and produce an answer.

"Like a log, thank you. And when I woke up and saw the view, well I just had to come out and be part of it. You didn't tell me it was going to be like this!"

"Didn't I?" His eyes twinkled as he looked up at her. "Maybe I was afraid that if I made it sound too idyllic you would come for all the wrong reasons. Besides it's not always like this. Sometimes we have hurricanes. In fact one of the first things you're going to have to learn about is the evacuation plan, and what to do if the siren sounds."

Claire looked at him in horror. "Are you serious?"

"'Fraid so. But we're a long way off hurricane season so you don't need to worry about it yet."

Thinking the onset of the hurricane season might be yet another good reason to return home when her six months were up, Claire dragged her eyes away from Daniel's upturned face, and particularly away from the generous curves of his grinning mouth, and turned her gaze back towards the beach.

"I'm just off to take a look at the white pelicans. Want to come with me?" The question was a casual one as Daniel readied himself to start up the engine.

Remembering the note from Beth she had found propped on the kitchen counter, Claire shook her head. "Another time. I need to unpack before Beth arrives."

He gave something that sounded like a snort or derision. "That's not any kind of an excuse. Beth won't be with you until ten, and the trip out to the sandbar will only take half-an-hour or so. Come on Claire, you've plenty of time. And early morning is the best part of the day to see them, before the boat trips start."

Knowing he would think her foolish, maybe even pathetic, Claire still searched for reasons why she couldn't join him. Her heart told her it was too soon. Later, when she had settled into her job, it would be fine. He would just be wallpaper by then. Someone she was used to being around. Now though, the sight of his laughing face and the curling ends of his dirt blond hair were causing her actual physical pain.

"I can't. I haven't even showered yet, and besides I haven't had breakfast."

"I won't tell if you don't. And I have enough breakfast for both of us." He nodded towards the rucksack. "Coffee, juice, fruit and bread."

Out of excuses, and knowing when she was beaten, Claire made her way to the ladder leading down to the mooring. By the time she reached the lowest rung he was holding the boat steady and waiting to help her. For once extremely grateful for her long legs, she ignored his outstretched hand and jumped, landing gracefully in the middle of the boat.

"You've done that before," he said with a nod of approval.

"Mmm. I spent a summer on the canals with my parents," she told him. "It was their maritime period! Dad wore an old sailor's cap all the time, and Mum dressed like a pirate, right down to the red bandana and striped T! Not exactly the open sea, of course, but it was the best they could manage. I had to secure the ropes at every lock, so I became quite good at jumping on and off moving boats."

"Sounds idyllic. Surely you enjoyed some of it." He had heard the disparagement in her voice and his face was serious as he untied the painter and pushed them clear of the pier.

The memories came flooding back as she heard the waves slapping against the prow. It was a long, long time since she had been in any sort of boat. Suddenly she remembered the freedom of that hot summer when her bare feet had become so tough she had been able to climb trees and walk across rough stones without flinching. It had been a summer when she had had only the most cursory relationship with hot water and a flannel, and had worn next to nothing for days on end until even her normally pale skin had turned biscuit brown in the sun. A summer of alfresco meals on riverbanks; of non-existent bedtimes; of watching the stars rock to and fro as she slept on the cabin roof with only her old dog Barney for company. To her surprise she was overcome with feeling of sadness. Where had it all gone, all that freedom? Why had she buried herself in a city and lived most of her adult life through books?

Her reply, when it came, was thoughtful. "A lot of it was really good. In fact it was probably what started my interest in photography. I was about ten years old and I remember I spent hours walking along the towpath picking wild flowers and searching for bugs and butterflies. I can remember getting really frustrated too because I couldn't draw well enough to record them. Then, one day, Dad disappeared for ages, and when he came back he had an old camera he'd found in a second-hand shop. I thought it was fantastic and…well I've never stopped taking pictures since. "

"There you go. You obviously benefited from your crazy childhood far more than you realize."

"I guess," Claire agreed. Then she changed the subject. She didn't want to think about her childhood anymore, particularly not now Daniel had made her feel guilty about her attitude towards her parents. After all, if she had a bit more of their adventurous spirit then visiting Dolphin Key and working with Daniel wouldn't be such a big deal.

Chapter Eight

They didn't say very much for a while after that. Daniel was too busy guiding the dinghy round the pier and out into the bay, and Claire was too busy absorbing everything that came into view. Only when she laughed out loud at the sight of at least twenty brown pelicans perched every which way on a derelict wooden structure that had collapsed into the sea, did Daniel speak.

"It's the local doss house," he told her with a grin. "Once upon a time it was part of an old landing stage but most of it disintegrated years ago. These guys took this bit over a few years back and now it's one of the iconic images of Dolphin Key. You'll see it everywhere. On postcards, books, posters...even on letterheads."

"I can see why. It's just so funny, and yet picturesque at the same time," Claire turned her head as he steered the dinghy away from the pelicans and their dilapidated roost.

"The white pelicans are a bit different," he told her, opening up the throttle in a noisy burst as they sped across the bay. "Much more stately; they are almost aristocracy compared to their common cousins."

But Claire had stopped listening to him. Instead she was looking over his shoulder, her eyes wide with disbelief. He turned his head to follow her gaze and was just in time to see a pod of dolphins flip into the air before arcing back into the sea.

"Hunting for breakfast," he said. "Same as the white pelicans will be. Everyone eats early around here."

After looking in vain for another sighting, Claire brought her gaze reluctantly back to the boat. Daniel smiled at her. "Your first time?"

She nodded.

"It gets everyone the same way. Soon you'll be used to it though. There are so many of them around here that before long you will start to recognize individual dolphins because they swim in a particular place at a regular time each day."

Claire stared at him. "Are you serious? This just gets more and more like fantasy land!"

He grinned at her. "You'd better believe it. Was I right that you will love living here?"

"Maybe."

Claire wasn't prepared to commit herself completely, not until she had met her colleagues and started work, but she had to admit that so far, if it weren't for the complication of how she felt about Daniel, then life in Dolphin Key would be close to heavenly. She turned to look for dolphins again and was rewarded, instead, by her first sight of the white pelicans. At the same time Daniel cut the throttle, and in a moment the only sounds were the slap of water against the boat and the squabble of the feeding birds. He let the dinghy drift in among the reeds fringing one of a string of tiny islands and threw out an anchor.

"Time for our breakfast too, although I can't offer you any choice." He leaned forward and pulled the rucksack towards him. In moments he had handed her a bottle of orange juice, a banana and a hunk of bread torn from a fresh loaf.

Claire took it gratefully. She hadn't realized how hungry she was until she saw the food. Now she tucked in greedily, not caring at all it was the sort of unsophisticated picnic she might have put together herself when she was about twelve years old.

* * *

As they watched the pelicans wheeling and diving in their search for food, Daniel told her a little about them. Then, when he noticed how focused she was, he stopped talking entirely and just let her watch them. He saw how she took in every detail and realized that it was her gift of concentration that made her a good photographer.

And she was good. He had seen what she could do because, although he had been desperate to find a way to keep seeing her despite the fact that there was an ocean between them, he hadn't been so besotted that he hadn't checked out her work before he offered her the job. If it hadn't been good enough he would have found another way, but it had turned out to be unnecessary. It had been easy to check too, because when they first met she had mentioned the names of a few publications that used her photos. They were nature magazines and a couple of local newspapers whose back numbers were available online. He had found them by searching the Internet and it had only taken him a few minutes to be impressed by the quality of her work. Now, watching her watch the pelicans, he could see why she was so good.

Her focus had another benefit too. It meant he could study her undisturbed, something that made him feel less like the stalker he had felt himself to be earlier. It hadn't been intentional, well not consciously anyway. He had always planned to visit the pelicans this morning, to check on their behavior in case they were preparing to migrate back to their nesting grounds in Canada. He had wanted to be sure Claire saw them before they went so she could get a few good shots that could be used on the company's promotional literature. It had never been his intention to take her with him today, so his glance towards her balcony as he tied up the dinghy had been no more than curiosity, a wish to see if the drapes were drawn back or whether she was still asleep. What he had seen, however, had arrested his hands midway through securing the dinghy to the pier, and he had had to grab hold of one of the wooden stanchions to stop the current sweeping him out into the bay again.

Claire had been standing on her balcony, leaning forward, one hand shading her eyes against the early morning brightness of a burgeoning sun that was sparking mahogany highlights in her cloud of black hair. Hair that was corkscrewing into a tangle of curls in front of him right now thanks to the salty dampness that still had to be burned out of the atmosphere.

It hadn't been her curls that had grabbed his attention though. It had been the outline of her body that had mesmerized him. Curving in all the right places and clad only in a T-shirt that just skimmed the top of her thighs, the pale shape of her long legs and bare feet were visible through the balcony railings. She was obviously totally unaware she was on public view, and in a way she was right because probably nobody else would have noticed her tucked away at the top of the apartment building, no one except him. He hadn't been able to take his eyes off her, however. He had tied up and then stayed in the dinghy, just watching her, until she had suddenly moved away and disappeared through the half open drapes.

It was only then he remembered what he had come for and had clambered up onto the pier and jogged down the road to collect his supplies. When he returned she was on the beach. Fully dressed now, and wearing sturdy trainers, she was trawling the tideline, pausing every now and then to poke at something with her toe or to pick it up for closer examination. Unable to stop himself he had stayed where he was, rucksack hooked over one shoulder, watching as she came slowly towards him.

By the time she reached the pier, however, commonsense had taken hold and he had clambered down into the dinghy. He couldn't hang around like a heartsick schoolboy forever. He had a job to do so the sooner he pushed his feelings for her into the background and got on with it the better. There would be plenty of time later to worry about what he was going to do about the flip his heart gave every time he saw her. She needed time to settle into her job before he could risk making a move. Until then he had to keep his distance, just be a work colleague, because from her reaction to him so far it was obvious that was exactly how she saw him.

Then she had stopped to look at the view at a point just above where his dinghy was moored, and all his good intentions had fled.

* * *

"They are stunning! I so wish I had brought my camera," Claire broke into his thoughts as she shifted round to look at him.

He smiled at her, banishing the effect her cool gray gaze had on his blood pressure. "In that case I'd better give you a crash course in dinghy management so that you can come out here any time you want. How are your boating skills?"

"Non existent! I told you, I was just the lock keeper."

He slid sideways to make room for her. "Well it's time you learnt then. You can take us back in."

Claire shook her head. This was becoming surreal. One moment she was a librarian putting in her hours at a city library, her only light relief the regular visits from local schoolchildren. The next she was watching pelicans squabble over pieces of fish while the early morning sun warmed her back, and while the man of her dreams stuffed the remains of their picnic back into his rucksack and talked casually about handing her the controls of his boat.

"I…are you sure about this?"

His nodded as he patted the seat beside him. "Come over here and I'll take you through it."

She clambered across to the stern, sat beside him, and watched carefully while he showed her how to lower the outboard motor back into the water and pull the throttle sufficiently hard to fire it up.

"Now your turn," he leaned back so that she could reach the tiller more easily, and then delivered a steady stream of encouragement as she tried to copy him. She was successful at her third attempt, and soon they were heading back towards the pier while the white pelicans patrolled the reeds behind them.

Claire felt her confidence grow as the dinghy responded to her lightest touch. Less than three months ago she would have laughed if anyone had told her she would be sailing across a small inlet in the Gulf of Mexico amongst dolphins and pelicans, instead of trudging to work through the cold winds and rain that were inevitable in February in northern Europe. Yet, somehow, it already felt like the most natural thing in the world. Exhilarated she turned to Daniel with a wide smile. A smile that faltered as their eyes met and for one long, long moment they stared at one another.

Feeling as if her heart was about to burst out of her body, she started to turn away. As she did so she saw the dolphins again.

Noticing them at the same time and realizing that they were swimming towards the dinghy, Daniel quickly took the tiller and slowed the engine until they were barely moving. Then they sat, side-by-side, watching, as a small group of dolphins frolicked across their stern. It wasn't until they had finally become no more than sleek shadows speeding away across they bay that Claire remembered to breathe.

Daniel chuckled as he opened up the throttle. "Over to you again if you're not too dolphin struck!"

She grinned at him as she took the tiller. "I can't believe I'll ever become blasé about them."

"Oh you will, believe me."

He pulled his gaze away from the mesmerizing effect of her wide, gray eyes. Eyes that were so thickly fringed with black lashes that they could be an advertisement for mascara, except that her face was scrubbed clean of makeup, reliant only on its own natural color and the flush the early morning sun had brought to her cheeks.

With an inward sigh he took his arm away from where it had rested behind her while they watched the dolphins, and shifted himself to the middle of the dinghy. For one brief moment, out there at the edges of the bay, he had thought that maybe she was attracted to him. There had been something in her eyes when she looked at him, something that had made his heart beat just that little bit faster, and then the dolphins had disturbed them. For the very first time in his life he wished they had just for once kept their acrobatics to themselves instead of showing off all around the boat.

Chapter Nine

For the next hour and a half Claire's morning was far more mundane as she showered and changed, unpacked her clothes, and generally familiarized herself with the apartment.

When she had returned from her unplanned boat trip she had been surprised to find that it was still only eight-thirty.

"I feel as if I've been up for hours already," she told Daniel as she deftly avoided his steadying hand and made a grab for the ladder as soon as he secured the dinghy.

"See you later," he called as he pulled the painter free and circled round at speed until he was pointing towards the open bay. Then he was gone in a splutter of noise that set the gulls in motion and rocked the sea into waves that slapped against the stanchions of the pier.

Claire watched him speeding across the bay for several minutes before she walked slowly back to her apartment, forcing herself to concentrate on the white pelicans and the dolphins so she didn't have to think about Daniel. It didn't work though. By the time she was in the shower the memory of his proximity returned with such a vengeance that she could recall, with a disturbing clarity, the way the early morning dampness lifted the ends of his hair into a tousle of half curls; the way his brown eyes glinted gold in the soft rays of the early morning sunshine, the way his strong fingers guided the boat, and then, later, directed her own hands on the tiller.

Determinedly she turned the faucet of the shower to cold and spent the next two minutes under a blast of water that left her breathless. Then, her skin rosy, and her hair dripping around her shoulders, she stepped from the shower and rubbed herself dry with the huge fluffy towel Beth had left hanging on the bath rail. She wasn't going to think about Daniel any more.

* * *

Beth arrived on the dot of ten. She greeted Claire with a wide smile and a bag of doughnuts.

"I thought these would wash down well with a mug of coffee," she said.

Claire returned her smile as she invited her into the apartment. Beth was small, with delicate features, tousled brown hair, and wide blue eyes. A baggy T-shirt over a pair of cotton cut-offs hid the pregnant curve of her stomach so effectively that she looked more like a carefree teenager than a mother-to-be. She saw Claire's gaze go instinctively to her midriff, however, and she laughed.

"I guess Daniel told you," she said.

He has a nice wife who is recently pregnant, Claire remembered Daniel's exact words and, even worse, she remembered exactly where they had been standing when he said them. They had been in the foyer of the hotel where they'd first met, and he'd been explaining why his brother had set up their date. A flush of embarrassment washed over her face as she nodded. At the same time she wondered why she had ever thought signing up to a dating agency was a good idea.

Beth plumped herself down into an armchair, placed the bag of donuts onto the coffee table, and grinned at her.

"Carl is a jerk," she said conversationally. Then she added, "he's my jerk and I love him. He's still a jerk though!"

"I…you know then…how Daniel and I met, I mean?"

"'Fraid so! Daniel didn't try to keep his voice down when he was bawling Carl out for interfering in his life."

She gave a peal of laughter when she saw Claire's stricken expression. "Hey don't look so tragic. Nobody over here is looking for any love interest between you two. We know Daniel invited you to join him for a meal because he felt he owed you one thanks to Carl, and when you got talking he discovered you were looking for a new job and realized he had exactly the right one on offer. "

"That's about it," Claire agreed.

She didn't know why Daniel hadn't gone into more detail, such as how he had tracked her down at work and infiltrated her family circle, how he had persisted with the job offer until he'd worn her down, but she was very grateful he hadn't.

Although she still didn't understand why he wanted her when it would have been easier to find someone suitable in America, she had given up trying to make sense of it. If he thought she was just what his organization needed and was prepared to smooth every obstacle in her path so she could move continents, then she was just going to make the most of the experience. She decided to put a lighthearted slant on the whole episode for Beth's benefit; a public joke that would counter any lingering suspicion she and Daniel were in anyway interested in one another.

"It was actually very funny. Daniel's face was a picture. He was so angry with his brother, and so embarrassed for me, that I...well I got the giggles!"

"Let me guess. That would be at about the same time Daniel had a sense of humour bypass!"

Claire grinned at her, and soon they were both convulsed with laughter. It was only later, when they'd finished their coffee and were about to leave the apartment that Beth put a slight damper on the morning.

"Carl is still far too pleased with himself," she said. "Daniel has been looking for the right person to join the team for ages, so the fact he landed you as a result of being set up on a date is a plus as far as my dear husband is concerned.

And that's about it, thought Claire gloomily as she followed Beth along the wooden walkway and down the stairs. I'm the right person for the team. There's nothing more to it than that, so the sooner I accept it, the better.

* * *

The weather was too good for her to feel gloomy for long, however. By the time they reached the street she was being warmed by the sun, while overhead the sky was a glorious unbroken blue. As they walked along Beth pointed out landmarks, giving her a potted history of some of the residents of Dolphin Cove along the way.

"Scott and Daniel will tell you more than you want to know about the nature reserve, and the birds and wildlife, but they won't ever get around to telling you about the things that really matter," she said, as they passed more shops and galleries than Claire had expected in such a small place. There also seemed to be far too many restaurants for a population of less than a thousand people. She guessed it was because Dolphin Cove was primarily a tourist resort

Beth interrupted her thoughts. "Here is our one and only supermarket. If it doesn't have what you want today, it will by tomorrow as long as you know the right people to ask. Come on in and I'll introduce you to Carol."

Carol, who was whippet thin, and who wore her dark hair pulled back into a tight ponytail, looked both upset and worried when she saw Beth. "You haven't come in for Mr Marchant's order have you? I phoned the supplier yesterday and he promised to send it but it wasn't on the delivery van this morning."

"Then he'll have to wait like the rest of us!" Beth was unsympathetic.

"That's all very well for you to say. You don't have to phone him up and tell him. Last time it arrived late he spent five minutes bawling me out." The other woman seemed close to tears.

"Well if he does it again just cut the call!"

"I can't do that!" She seemed genuinely horrified at the suggestion.

"Yeah, you can, and if he doesn't like it then he'll have to find another way to buy his smelly cigars. He's a cranky old man who enjoys upsetting everyone. If more people stood up to him, then perhaps he'd start to be a bit nicer all round."

She turned to Claire with an apologetic smile. "As you've probably realized by now, my dear father-in-law isn't my most favourite person. He lost his sight a few years back and he's been taking it out on everyone else ever since, including Carol, whose family has been looking after the Marchants for years."

Carol forgot her own worries and gave Claire a wide smile. "I guess you're the person who's joining Daniel's eco company."

"She is. And, luckily for her, she won't have to have anything to do with the old man because unlike poor Daniel, she's not working in the family business as well."

* * *

Claire left a grocery order with Carol and promised to tell her if she ever wanted anything that wasn't stocked on the overflowing shelves. Then they left her to chase up her late orders and walked slowly up the main street while Beth ticked off the other establishments she thought might be useful.

"There's the post office," she said, pointing. "It closes twelve 'til two and it's not open weekends. The one and only bank is next door. And that blue building is the bookshop. Only go in there if you have an hour or more to spare because Tom Cook, who runs it, doesn't let anyone out until he's told them his life history! And just across the street is the hairdresser. Not that you're going to need to go there very often," she added as she looked admiringly at Claire's thick black curls."

Laughing at Beth's description of what was to be her home for at least the next six months, Claire finally managed to ask the question that had been intriguing her ever since they left the supermarket.

"Is Mr Marchant senior really that bad?"

"Worse!" Beth's reply was swift and to the point. "His mother is a love though, or at least she was until recently. Now she's just depressed. I think she's so worn down by the old fiend's bullying she's sort of given up."

"And what about the rest of the family?"

"Oh they've all escaped. Well the twins have because they are away at college for most of the year, and Sarah is married and lives in Texas. And as my father-in-law has made it very clear Carl and I are not welcome, we never visit, so that just leaves Daniel."

"How does he cope?"

Beth gave her a sharp look. "You'll find out soon enough. In the meantime, we've arrived."

Not sure whether she had been reprimanded for being too nosey, or whether Beth had merely lost interest in the conversation, Claire followed her along a path that meandered in a haphazard fashion across half an acre of rough grass. It ended at a low wooden building set amongst trees and shrubs. Painted a soft green, it merged with the foliage surrounding it. The door stood wide, and all the windows were open.

"Here we are at last!" Beth announced to what appeared to be an empty office. Her words were greeted by a moment's silence followed by a series of bumps and thumps, and then a loud oath as a man crawled out from beneath a desk. He rubbed his head and stood up. He was dressed in dark shorts and a green T bearing a company logo.

He grinned at Claire and stuck out his hand. "Sorry about that! The computer is on the blink. I'm Scott. Welcome aboard!"

Hoping that her jaw hadn't actually dropped open, Claire took his hand with a dazed smile because he was, without doubt, one of the most beautiful men she had ever seen. About Daniel's height, but broader, he obviously worked out regularly. And his olive skin, dark hair, strong cleft chin and perfect teeth made him the hero of every romantic novel she had ever read.

An hour later, logged onto a new laptop computer and surrounded by piles of leaflets and company reports, Claire watched Scott making coffee in the tiny storeroom that doubled as a kitchen, and wondered anew at her good fortune. An apartment on the beach, early morning assignations with pelicans and dolphins, and now a work colleague whose film star looks were combined with a sweet nature and an enthusiasm for his job that left her breathless.

His stunning looks could have turned him into the sort of man who considered it his divine right to have all women at his beck and call. He could have been a nightmare to work with. Instead, he was friendly and down to earth, apparently ready to turn his hand to anything, including making the coffee. All she had to learn to do was to stop staring at him so that he didn't get the wrong idea. It was going to be very difficult though, because her photographer's eye was already conjuring up a thousand and one poses for the company's publicity material. If Daniel was trying to widen its appeal then Scott was his man. Leaflets with a picture of him on the front would draw in every female tourist within miles of Dolphin Key.

"I didn't tell you that the job had a hidden bonus, did I?" Beth whispered wickedly as she dumped yet another pile of papers on Claire's desk. "And he's single too. No complicated past. No girlfriends that I know of. So as that date with Daniel didn't work out, you're both completely fancy-free. How lucky is that!"

Their eyes met and they both dissolved into giggles, which they struggled to hide as Scott came out of the kitchen carrying three mugs of coffee. Taking hers, Claire thanked him without daring to look at Beth. Even though they had only met that morning, they already understood one another perfectly. Sisters under the skin, she thought, and she was suddenly very glad she had made the move to Florida.

It *was* time she got out more, did something with her life. Like Wendy in Peter Pan, which had always been her favourite childhood story, it was time she learned to fly. If she got shot down by an arrow to the heart, then so what? The wound would heal and she would just have to get up and try again.

Chapter Ten

Claire spent the rest of the day either being briefed by Scott or forced to concentrate on various administrative functions by Beth.

"I know I can't compete but this stuff is really important," she complained when Claire's attention was diverted yet again by Scott dropping another report onto her desk. "You need to know where I file everything, how the expenses system works, who you need to talk to if there's an emergency, all that sort of thing, or you won't be able to function on the days when I'm not here."

Scott hastily retrieved the report from Claire's desk and shoved it into his top drawer. "Sorry! Sorry! Sorry! She's right. I'll grab some sandwiches for us while you two discuss all the boring stuff!"

Beth threw a screwed up ball of paper at his retreating back and then turned to Claire. "I don't come in on Wednesdays or Fridays because that's when I help Carl at the print shop. All the major stuff can wait until I'm here of course, but there will still be things you'll have to deal with such as queries from the public, or where to find a particular document."

Claire gave Beth her full attention. "I didn't realize. I guess I just thought you worked here while Carl ran his own business. I didn't know there was an overlap."

"That would be far too simple and straightforward for the Marchant family," Beth told her. "No, Carl runs his own print design business, and I share my time between him and Daniel, that's when I'm not acting as a buffer between them and their father!"

Remembering her bitter remarks earlier in the day Claire decided to steer the conversation towards Carl rather than his father. "What sort of design work does he do?"

"All the basic stuff, letterheads, leaflets, posters, that sort of thing. Most of the local businesses use him now although it took us a while to persuade them. And Daniel uses him too of course, so you'll be working with him once you start to revamp some of these leaflets with your photos."

She saw the panicked expression on Claire's face and grinned. "Don't worry. He won't mention THAT date! Not if he knows what's good for him anyway."

Claire gave a relieved laugh. "He seems to have dug himself into a deep hole with you as well as Daniel over that."

"You better believe it! Now are you going to let me take you through the admin system or not?"

"I'm all yours," Claire assured her as she turned her back on the stuff Scott had given her and moved her chair across to Beth's desk.

* * *

The rest of the day passed quickly, especially when, after a hurried lunch of shared sandwiches, Scott took Claire through the program of events he had penciled into the calendar for forthcoming year. Fascinated by such items as *Horseshoe Crab Bonanza, Down Upon the Suwanee River* and *Runway Eagles,* none of which meant anything at all to her, she realized that she had a great deal to learn about the place that was to be her home for at least the next few months.

She and Scott were still discussing some of the details when Daniel finally turned up. Not aware she had an audience, Claire was making a robust case for a change to one of the puzzle books that had been produced for children.

"Photographs would make it so much more interesting. These line drawings are good but they don't have the punch of an actual picture. Children are fine with drawn illustrations in story books but when it's factual stuff they want real pictures of the things they're learning about."

"Told you she knew her stuff!" Daniel walked across the room and picked up a copy of the booklet they were talking about, chuckling as he did so.

Scott nodded. "It's exactly what I need. A challenge. No more *do what you think is best Scott, because we are all too busy to listen to you.*"

"Are they really that bad?" Claire joined in with the banter.

"Worse!" Scott told her. Then he cleared his desk by scooping all the papers into his drawer with one sweep of his arm. "They're quite good drinking companions though. Who's for a beer?"

"Not me, I've got a house to run," Beth had tidied her own desk and now she picked up her bag and made for the door.

"As if!" Scott jeered at her retreating back. "Everyone knows Carl does all the ironing and the cooking. You're probably going home to drape yourself across the sofa and watch him stir saucepans."

"Ah yes but I'm going to drape in a very supportive way," she grinned at them all, blew a kiss, and was gone.

"How about you Claire?" Scott asked as he pushed back his chair, stood up and stretched. "Can we welcome you to Dolphin Cove with a celebratory drink."

Claire glanced at her watch. "I don't really have the time. I promised Carol I would pick up my groceries before the supermarket closes."

"Not a problem, we can do that on the way. In fact I'll even carry them home for you as long as you don't tell Beth. I don't want her to think my male chauvinist tendencies have softened."

"In that case…"

"I can do better than that. I have transport or, to be more precise, Claire has transport," Daniel interrupted, suddenly wondering if putting Claire and Scott together had been such a good idea after all. It was one thing for work colleagues to get on well, entirely another when they got on too well. He hoped that wasn't about to happen here before he made a move of his own. Surely Claire would see Scott for what he was. A great guy, a good worker, but emotionally on the shallow side. Someone who appeared to want a good time without any responsibilities, and someone whose looks and physique ensured that he usually managed to get it.

Banishing such uncharitable thoughts, he smiled at Claire's questioning look. "Come and take ownership of your company car," he said.

Gathering up her bag and sweater, she followed him outside to where a customized green and yellow golf cart was parked. It had the company logo on the side panel. Daniel grinned at her stunned expression.

"Carts are mainly what everyone uses around here so the town doesn't get clogged up with cars and trucks. Even the police use their own version for local patrol. It will only do twenty kilometers an hour max but that's not a problem in a place this size. Also it doesn't pollute, and it's quiet, both things that are very useful for us when we're anywhere near a wildlife habitat."

Claire gave a disbelieving shake of the head. "This place gets more and more surreal by the minute, but I love it."

He handed her the keys. "I'll talk you through it. It's really easy to drive but you must remember to follow all the normal traffic rules."

Claire gave a joyous laugh as she turned on the ignition. Memories of the summer her father had decided to take up golf flooded back to her. Memories of early mornings full of bird song, of wild flowers growing along the edges of the greens, of rabbits, and squirrels, and an occasional fox, and of the exhilaration of being in total charge of her father's golf buggy even though she was only thirteen years old.

"Come on! What are you waiting for?" She swung the buggy in a wide arc so that it was pointing downtown, back towards the supermarket.

"You're obviously way ahead of me on this," Daniel said as he jumped into the passenger seat with a smile of approval. Not to be outdone, Scott swung in behind with a loud whoop of enthusiasm, and the three of them drove down the road at a steady ten kilometers an hour. When they reached the supermarket Claire parked the golf cart with a flourish to the joint applause of her passengers.

Sending a silent thank you to her father, she grinned at them before hurrying into the shop to collect her groceries.

* * *

Two beers, a tuna salad, and three pages of the book she was reading later, and Claire was sound asleep, her bedside light still burning. It had been a very long day!

* * *

Too tired to be seriously affected by jet lag, Claire slept without waking until six o'clock the following morning. Then, resisting the temptation with some difficulty, she showered and dressed before she pulled back the drapes and stepped out onto the balcony. As if they had been waiting for her, a group of dolphins immediately flipped into action and chased one another across the bay. The water streaming from their backs turned to iridescent silver in the early morning sun. Transfixed, she watched them until they disappeared, and then hurriedly prepared her breakfast and spent the next thirty minutes sitting on the balcony wondering what she had done to deserve such an idyllic start to her day.

Watching dolphins while I eat breakfast and drink freshly squeezed orange juice she texted to Jenny, hoping that would be sufficiently exotic to distract her friend from her self-imposed role as marriage broker. She had already sent Claire a stream of messages, most of them asking whether she and Daniel were an item yet.

Just as well she doesn't know about the beautiful Scott or I'd never get any peace at all, Claire smiled to herself as she pressed the send button. Then she collected her belongings and set off for her second working day.

* * *

It started with Scott suggesting they visit the local Wildlife Refuge. "I know you've lots of reading to do," he said. "But it's not the same as actually seeing the birds in their own habitat. You need to do it several times in succession, and at different times in the day, so that you develop a feel for the place."

"Does that mean I get to sail the dinghy again?" Claire asked.

He gave her a startled look. "Have you been out in it already?"

"Well yes…Daniel took me out to look at the white pelicans yesterday morning. Didn't he say?"

"No, but no matter. At least you've seen them already so I can concentrate on showing you some of the other wildlife that's out there. And yes, you will get to sail the dinghy again, because you need to become proficient enough to take it out on your own. This week is not too bad but soon the place will be so overloaded with tourists we'll be lucky to find time enough to talk to one another, let alone spend a whole morning together at the Refuge."

* * *

Beth was too involved with a series of phone calls to acknowledge the fact they were leaving the office together, so when Daniel arrived forty minutes later she didn't have the slightest idea where they'd gone.

"They might have gone to the islands," she guessed. "Or maybe Scott is just showing her around the area."

Thwarted in his attempt to see the woman who had invaded his dreams so badly the previous night that he had eventually given up all pretense of sleeping and been out in his boat well before sunrise, Daniel looked for something to do. None of the hundred and one jobs that were waiting for him held any appeal. Nor did the prospect of hanging around until Scott and Claire returned. He didn't want to see them rosy-cheeked and full of a joint enthusiasm for whatever adventure they had been involved in, not now he had started to worry about how well they seemed to be getting along.

Why hadn't he given Scott a thought when he had moved heaven and earth to get Claire to Dolphin Key? How could he have been that stupid? How could he have placed her in an everyday situation with someone who, he knew from the gossip he had picked up from Beth, was so high up there in the male attraction stakes that he was like a walking, talking babe magnet. And as far as he could tell, Scott milked it for all he was worth, the same as any red-blooded man would unless he was hooked on a tall slim woman with a cloud of blue-black hair and an enchanting dimple at the corner of her mouth.

In the past Daniel had seen Scott work a room full of female tourists to such effect that the organization was better off to the tune of several hundred dollars by the time he had finished. At the time he had found it amusing, but now that he was worried Scott might target Claire, he didn't feel like laughing one little bit.

"Are you okay?" Beth peered at him over the top of the glasses she wore when she was working.

"I'm fine," he said. "Just tell Scott I'll come back later on this afternoon so we can go over the figures for the work we're doing with the university."

"But..." Beth didn't finish what she was about to say. Instead she watched his retreating back in puzzlement. He and Scott had already been over the figures and agreed them. The bidding letter had gone to the Marine Research Department at the university over a week ago. What was to discuss!

Then she shrugged. She was used to Daniel. He always had too much to do, was always trying to keep too many balls in the air, so maybe it wasn't surprising if he dropped one occasionally.

* * *

Claire, meanwhile, was having the time of her life. Despite having the normal female appreciation of his sensational good looks, she was completely immune to Scott's charms thanks to her hang-up on Daniel. Consequently she was enjoying the trip out to the cluster of islands that made up the wildlife nature refuge far more than she had the previous day. For a start she wasn't self-conscious every time her eyes met Scott's, nor did she become tense if his hand brushed against hers, or if his long legs, clad in khaki shorts, bumped against her as he leaned across the dinghy to correct her steering.

"Sorry!" he would tell her cheerfully, and then continue to explain about the wildlife they were looking at, were going to see, or had already seen.

And Claire, who had never seen so many birds in once place in her life, would just smile at him, or ask questions, or jot down a sentence or two in the notebook she had stuffed into her pocket as they left the office.

She liked Scott and she knew the feeling was reciprocated. She also knew there would never be a glimmer of romance between them. The necessary zing of attraction just wasn't there. They were on the same wavelength as far as work was concerned, however. They were both passionate about wildlife education; both full of ideas; and they each recognized the other as a useful sounding board, someone to discuss things with, make plans with. It all filled her with excitement. At last she had found something she really wanted to do. If only she could get her feelings for Daniel into perspective, then life would be perfect.

Chapter Eleven

When Daniel reappeared Beth was already packing up to go home. She had passed on his message to Scott, who had shrugged good-naturedly and then carried on talking to Claire. Now she watched them and smiled as she wondered if there was any chance their working relationship would eventually lead to romance. They were ideally suited after all. Both of them were passionate about their work. Both of them were focused and intelligent, and both of them were completely unaware of the effect their looks had on the people around them.

Admittedly Scott played the field from time to time, but Beth knew his heart wasn't really in it. He was too wrapped up in his precious wildlife, and far too keen to get up before dawn to watch for migrating birds to consider settling down with a permanent girlfriend.

It was too soon to understand Claire of course, but she would love to know her back history. Not that she expected to learn about it anytime soon because there was something innately private about her. Also, if Daniel was to be believed, she wasn't interested in dating, although why she would have told him that Beth couldn't begin to understand. After all they had met via an Internet dating site, so she must have been looking for someone. Maybe she was suffering from a recently broken heart, or some other emotional trauma that would slowly heal around Scott. It was obvious that she liked him, so perhaps he would be the one to change her mind...except there didn't seem to be any sort of a spark between them. Beth's sensitive emotional antennae hadn't detected the slightest hint of flirtation so far.

True Claire's mouth had nearly hit her chin in amazed admiration when she first saw Scott, but the fit of giggles that had followed hadn't indicated any sort of romantic interest. Nor did she look as if she were smitten now. She just looked interested in what he was saying.

"Why don't you come down to the print shop tomorrow? It's my day to work with Carl so if you come down around lunchtime I'll be able to introduce you." Beth interrupted their discussion because she wanted to be able to talk about her matchmaking theories with Carl, and she couldn't do that until he'd met Claire. Besides, the sooner Claire met him and realized that he really wasn't going to say a word about the dating agency, the sooner she would lose that look of panic whenever his name was mentioned.

Her eyes met Claire's and their conspiratorial smiles were not lost on Scott. He was still trying to find out what their secret was when Daniel came through the door. Seeing the three of them so cheerful and relaxed in one another's company, he felt a twist of jealousy lodge in his heart. If only he didn't have to run the family business then he could spend all day working with them too. All day with Claire!

"Good day?" he asked her, trying hard to ignore the unhappiness that was threatening to overwhelm him.

"Very good," Claire admitted, wondering why he looked so terrible. He looked, she thought, like someone who has just had very bad news and was still trying to come to terms with it. The others didn't seem to notice anything amiss, however. Beth just picked up her bag and made her usual breezy exit, while Scott started to bombard him with questions about a project that was behind schedule.

She took advantage of their conversation to sort out her desk. So far she seemed to have spent more time out of the office than in it, and it was beginning to show. Beth appeared to have relocated a couple of smooth rocks from the path outside to weigh down the growing pile of paper on Claire's desk, but other than that the packets of pencils and pens were still unopened, and several notebooks were jumbled into the middle of some torn cellophane. There were several reports too, each at least a hundred pages thick, plus a separate pile of admin forms that she still had to complete.

Preoccupied with her own affairs, she didn't notice that Scott was leaving until he called out from the doorway. Raising her arm in a belated farewell she was suddenly aware that she was alone with Daniel; a Daniel who still looked poleaxed.

"Are you okay?" she asked before she could stop herself.

He started to say yes and then changed his mind. "Not really."

She waited, sensing that he was struggling with himself, and with his habit of keeping everything close to his chest. Her silence was his undoing.

"There's been a fire in one of our holiday developments in Mexico. Fortunately nobody was hurt although a couple of guests were sent to hospital as a precaution, but now I've got to go there. I'm booked onto the first flight out tomorrow."

"That's awful!" Claire's eyes grew wide with horror.

Having started to unburden himself, Daniel didn't seem able to stop. "It gets worse! I already had finance meetings booked back-to-back in London and New York to discuss some investment problems, so I'm going to be spread pretty thin over the next week or two. No more early morning visits to the islands I'm afraid. Nor to any of the other places I wanted to show you. You're going to have to rely on Scott and Beth to ease you into the job."

"That's the least of your problems," Claire's voice was soft with concern. "Is there anything I can do to help? Anything at all?"

He shook his head. "Thanks, but no. Scott and Beth will keep things ticking over here.

They're used to me being away. Besides they know that they can always contact me if necessary."

She nodded as she gathered up her belongings. She was sure that Daniel would want to be alone in the office to write instructions for Beth and Scott, and to update himself on the work program, so she was surprised when he stood up as well.

"Actually...maybe there is something," he said slowly. "It's a bit unorthodox...but would you come and meet my parents...my mother actually..."

Clare stared at him as his voice trailed off.

"I will if you really want me to but I don't understand why."

He gave a grim smile. "Of course you don't and I shouldn't ask, not really. It's just that I think...hope...that meeting someone new will cheer her up."

Seeing the same bleak expression on his face she had seen in her mother's kitchen all those weeks ago, Claire took a deep breath. "I know she isn't well...that is...Beth told me she's...depressed."

"I'd say it was despair rather than depression," he told her. "Over the past five years she's become so worn down emotionally and physically that she has no energy left for anything except caring for my father. She doesn't go out, doesn't read. She doesn't even tend her garden anymore. Her friends have more or less given up on her too because, although my father hates to be left on his own, he makes himself as unpleasant as possible if they visit."

"So why me?"

Suddenly he smiled, and it was like the sun coming out from behind the clouds. "Because she doesn't know you and nothing, not even her deep unhappiness, will stop her from being the perfect hostess. If you visit her then she will have to rally, even if it's just for an hour or so. Her good manners won't allow anything else!"

"Well if you're sure it'll help, then of course I'll come with you," Claire couldn't help smiling in return. "After all I owe you one for the way you charmed *my* parents."

"He had the grace to look a tiny bit embarrassed. "I was a bit pushy wasn't I?"

"Just a bit," she confirmed, and then laughed. "It made their weekend though."

"Mine too," he told her, his face suddenly serious. "I really enjoyed that weekend Claire, even though I didn't think I would ever crack your resolve to turn me down. Your parents, the life they lead, their happiness with one another, the way they don't interfere with your life, it was...I was...envious I suppose. "

Their eyes met, and for one long moment Claire forgot to breathe as memories of that fateful weekend assailed her and she felt the full force of his attraction all over again. This was what she had been afraid of. Yet she didn't have the heart to refuse his request to visit his parents, even though she knew she was opening herself up to all kinds of pain, because his worried expression tugged at her heartstrings in a way that his usual cheerful and practical manner never would.

* * *

It took longer to reach the Marchant's family home than Claire had expected because it was out beyond the curve of Dolphin Bay, and several kilometers past the local airfield. From a distance the airfield looked like a perfectly ordinary patch of rough grass. It was only when they drew close that Claire saw there was an airstrip marching alongside the road.

Instead of bypassing it, Daniel drove across the grass, stopped under a stand of tall pine and pointed. At the top, perched precariously, was an untidy nest of sticks. Sitting on it was an osprey, its expression imperious as it scanned the surrounding countryside.

"She comes back every year," Daniel told her. "Why she likes the airstrip rather than the Reserve we have no idea. It seems to work though. She raises a brood of chicks every time. So far she hasn't lost one."

Taking the binoculars he handed her, Claire watched in fascination as the bird stood up, turned around, and then settled back onto her nest.

In turn, Daniel watched Claire, absorbing the warmth of her skin so close to his, enjoying the moment as he pushed his troubles into the background. She was so unconscious of her

125

unusual beauty, so unaware of the effect she had on people. He had noticed Scott's expression of appreciation when they had gone for a beer the previous evening, noticed, too, the way her striking looks had drawn glances from most people in the bar. So why was she still single, so uninterested in dating? He wished he knew.

He was still watching her when she lowered the binoculars and turned to him. As their eyes met he forced himself to switch back to tour guide mode. He pointed to the osprey.

"They are sometimes called the fish eagle," he told her. "They love the shallow waters around Dolphin Key because it's easy fishing, so we get a lot of them."

Claire hurriedly put the binoculars back to her eyes. This was getting more difficult by the minute. Although she was sorry he had so many problems to deal with, maybe it was good he was going to be away for a while. It would give her a chance to get to know Dolphin Key without the added complication of a pounding heart, a dry mouth, and an inexplicable catch in her breath every time she was near him.

* * *

The Marchant family home was set back off a quiet road shaded by tall cypress trees, each one trailing a gray beard of Spanish moss. As the golf cart trundled up the driveway Claire realized that the back of the house overlooked the gulf.

"What a wonderful place to live," she gasped. "It must have been fantastic to grow up here."

"Sometimes it was," Daniel agreed as he turned off the ignition and stared at the building in front of him. He seemed about to say something else, but then he shrugged.

"Come inside. I expect my mother will be in the kitchen."

He was right. A tall, thin woman, whose hair was fading from blonde to silver, she was staring out of the window of a large kitchen that had beautifully crafted granite counters and a red oakwood floor.

"Mum, I've brought someone to see you," Daniel's voice was gentle.

She turned around with a start of surprise and Claire was shocked by the misery in her eyes. Then it was gone as she visibly pulled herself together and smiled.

"You must be Claire. Daniel told me you were going to join his team," her voice was cultured, her movements graceful as she walked across the kitchen with her hand outstretched.

Claire took it and was overwhelmed by the other woman's fragility. Clasping her hand was like holding a dry leaf. It felt brittle, insubstantial, as if it might break.

"I was showing Claire around and we happened this way," Daniel lied, avoiding Claire's eyes.

"And I don't suppose either of you have eaten yet." Fragile she might be but Mrs

Marchant's comment was entirely maternal, a mother who knew her son's habits, and whose instinct was to nurture.

Not waiting for an answer she turned to the stove where saucepans were simmering. "I'm cooking chicken and rice for your father and me but there's more than enough for both of you because I'm cooking a double portion. I was going to freeze it for another day."

"In that case we'd love to stay," Daniel gave Claire a questioning look.

She nodded. "If you're sure it's not too much trouble."

"Not at all. It will be nice to have some company. Now pour a drink for our guest Daniel and then take her out onto the deck until dinner is ready."

Claire started to protest, to suggest that she help the tired woman who was Daniel's mother. Then she stopped herself. Mrs Marchant didn't look as if she would welcome the sort of casual domesticity that was the norm in Claire's mother's kitchen. This was going to be a formal meal, with formal conversation. Nothing alfresco about it at all!

* * *

The dinner was exactly as Claire had anticipated and yet she enjoyed it because, true to Daniel's prediction, his mother rallied. A perfect hostess, she asked questions that were not too intrusive, and then listened intently to the answers. She entertained with stories of Dolphin Key; she talked about her one visit to Europe; she smiled and offered more food, more wine, and desert.

Her husband was an entirely different proposition however. Although he was courteous enough when he was introduced to Claire, he maintained a brooding silence throughout the meal, only speaking when he wanted more rice or when his glass needed refilling. After several unsuccessful attempts to include him in the conversation, Daniel gave up and concentrated on Claire, joining in with his mother's stories, making her laugh. Only Mrs Marchant persisted, ignoring every snub and acting as if every dismissive grunt was just a normal part of the conversation. Watching her attempt to include him, Claire felt desperately sorry for her.

"Do you have a Talking Books Service in Dolphin Key?" her question, asked in a lull in the conversation, was a blunt attempt to engage the man sitting at the head of the table. If she could talk to him about books, find some sort of common ground that would move them away from the topics that were obviously boring him, then the desperation might fade from Mrs Marchant's eyes.

Her question was followed by a long silence. For a moment she thought he hadn't heard her and she was about to repeat it when she caught sight of his wife's face. Mrs Marchant looked horrified. Daniel, sitting opposite Claire, put down his desert spoon as he waited for his father to reply. When no answer was forthcoming he pushed back his chair in disgust.

"Florida has an excellent Talking Books Service," he told her. "Unfortunately my father doesn't like it. Instead he prefers that my mother read to him."

Suddenly she understood. Her innocent question was a direct acknowledgement that Mr Marchant could no longer see, and his blindness was something nobody ever spoke about. This proud man, whose sightless eyes looked like milky brown buttons under a lowering brow, never admitted publically that he was blind. Instead he had made his wife complicit, forcing her to pretend everything was okay. She took a deep breath.

"Well I think that's a real shame," she said, steadfastly continuing to direct her conversation to the silent man at the head of the table. "There must be so many hours when she is too busy to read to you. What do you do then?"

"I sit and think young lady," when he finally answered her, his voice was husky, as if he didn't use it very often. He was a handsome man whose iron gray hair had once been dark, and whose loose limbed body was as tall as Daniel's. His features were different though. His face was sharp; almost hawk like, with discontented grooves on either side of his mouth, and a fierce furrow between his brows.

"What do you think about?" she asked him.

He gave a snort of derision as he carefully returned his wine glass to the table before he gestured around the room. "Not that it's any business of yours, but I think about work. Real work. The sort of work that brings in the money to support all of this, not the airy-fairy stuff Daniel does in his spare time."

Ignoring his implied criticism of her involvement with Daniel's organization, Claire soldiered on.

"I guess that means you like reading biographies, with perhaps crime thrillers for light relief."

He turned towards her with such a surprised expression on his face that Claire had to remind herself he couldn't see her.

"And what makes you think that?"

"Experience. I *am* a librarian after all. I know what people like to read, even though I have decided to take a break from the public library service to concentrate on some of the airy fairy stuff for a while!"

The silence that followed was unexpectedly broken by a bark of laughter. "Touché! Well in that case why don't you tell me what biographies I ought to read and then I'll tell you I've already read them!"

"If you like," Claire glanced at Daniel. He was smiling.

Mr Marchant pushed his chair back from the table and stood up. His wife immediately rushed to his side, ready to lead him into the sitting room where she was going to serve coffee. He brushed her aside.

"Daniel's young lady can take me. It seems we have a lot to talk about."

Daniel watched Claire lead his father across the room with something close to amazement. He had long ago given up hope of anyone getting through to him and yet somehow she had managed it. He wasn't sure whether he should be pleased or not because if anyone could turn Claire against having anything to do with the Marchant family, it was his father. Then he heard what Claire was saying as she and his father disappeared into the sitting room and acknowledged afresh that his father's rude and erratic behaviour was the least of his challenges.

"And for the record, I'm not Daniel's young lady, Mr Marchant. My name is Claire Harris and I'm just one of his employees," she said.

Chapter Twelve

Daniel was thoughtful as he arrived back at his own waterfront property. Built on stilts in the ubiquitous clapboard style, it was much smaller than his parent's house and without the high ceilings and wood beams. Instead it was open plan, and sparsely furnished with wooden tables and chairs, a well-worn saggy couch, and sailcloth cushions and drapes. Whitewashed walls, rush matting and a scattering of interesting pieces of wood and unusual shells gave it character, while a wall full of rough hewn shelves crammed with books, reports and piles of paper reflected his busy life. A half built boat took up most of the open space under the house, and in front of it, tied to a small wooden dock, was another boat and a yellow inflatable.

Climbing out of the golf cart he walked to the water's edge. The full moon was so bright it cast a silver path across the bay. At his feet the waves whispered and sighed where they met the sand. For the first time in a long time it all failed to soothe him.

Instead of absorbing the view he found himself reliving an evening where he had watched in growing admiration as Claire pitted her wits against his father and won. Sure that she wouldn't have heard of half the authors he enjoyed, the old curmudgeon had deliberately quoted name after name, only to discover she knew them all.

"I cheated," she told Daniel as he drove her back to her apartment block. "I didn't tell him I studied American Literature at university."

He roared with laughter. "Serves him right!"

Then, more seriously, he had tried to thank her. "You were great! I didn't mean for the visit to take up all your time though. Can you forgive me for hijacking your entire evening?"

She shrugged as she gave him that steady gray gaze, the one that put a considerable strain on his blood pressure. "It's not a problem,"

Then she'd paused in the act of stepping down from the golf cart and turned back with a half smile. "I hope it did what it was intended to do and took your mind off your worries about your mother for an hour or so."

Already out of the cart, he'd moved swiftly to her side. "It did, and thank you."

She nodded, but before she could turn away he grabbed her hand. "There aren't any words, Claire, to explain how good it was to see my parents interacting normally for once."

"Then I guess we're quits," she said. "Because we can't exactly pretend that my parents were a walk in the park either can we?"

They had stared at one another as they both remembered their weekend together and then they were laughing, and Claire's was the same laughter that had so intoxicated him when they first met. Full-throated peals punctuated with helpless giggles. Unable to stop himself he'd pulled her close.

"Quits indeed," he murmured and then he'd kissed her.

* * *

Now, remembering that kiss, remembering the softness of her skin, the scent of her shampoo, the slenderness of her fingers entwined with his, Daniel's body reacted anew. With a pang he remembered how empty he had felt when she pulled away from him, still laughing, and ran across the moonlit grass to the walkway leading to her apartment.

Thank goodness she had though. If she hadn't then he wouldn't have stopped at one chaste kiss, a kiss that could just about be mistaken for gratitude instead of desire; a kiss that had come out of nowhere, and which he wanted to repeat as soon as possible.

With a sigh he turned back to the house to begin the weary task of packing. It was far too soon to reveal how he felt about her. She needed time to settle into Dolphin Cove, into her job. If he confessed he'd offered her a job so they could get to know one another better, if he told her he hoped that she could learn to love him, then she would probably run a mile. Besides, there would be no time to think of her at all in the forthcoming days as he tried to sort out the increasing problems of the family business. For the immediate future he had to push all thoughts of romance to the back of his mind. He had absolutely no choice given the recent fire in Mexico and the finance meetings already set up in New York and London. It was a decision that made a very poor bedfellow as he tossed and turned and watched his alarm clock tick away the hours until it was time to get up, shower, and leave Claire and Dolphin Key behind him.

* * *

Claire, meanwhile, was having her own problems. Pushing open the double doors to her balcony she stood outside for a long time, letting the soft evening breeze cool her flushed cheeks as she relived the whisper soft touch of Daniel's mouth on hers. Why had he done that? Why had he spoiled a perfectly good evening by kissing her? There was no way she would be able to survive her six-month contract if he insisted on introducing casual affection into their working relationship. She had coped with it this time by twisting her head away from him and laughing, when what she had actually wanted to do was something far more intimate. Next time she might not be able to do that. Next time she might interpret a grateful goodnight kiss between friends as something more than he had intended and embarrass them both. Irritated by her reaction to something she knew meant nothing to Daniel, she eventually slammed the screen doors shut behind her and went to bed.

* * *

Fortunately the next few days did a lot to take her mind off how she felt about Daniel, and it wasn't just because he wasn't around to around to remind her, it was because her new job kept her so busy that she didn't have time to think about anything else but work. Not that it really seemed like work, or at least not like the nine to five slog she had endured for the past six years.

Her crowded bus journey had been replaced by a stroll down Main Street via a stop off at the pier, a stroll that soon had her on first name terms with the early morning fisherman, and on nodding terms with most of the shop and office workers she met en route. Thanks to Scott, it wasn't long before she was also welcomed by name in most of the inns and bars that overlooked the bay as well.

"Everyone is just so friendly," she told him the morning she arrived at work clutching a carefully wrapped fresh fish; a present from one of her newfound friends.

He laughed at her. "It doesn't take much to win you over does it?"

She smiled at him; not expecting him to understand the effect living in Dolphin Key was having on her. After years of commuting daily across a city where fellow travellers rarely spoke, where shop assistants were impersonal, and where few people knew even their nearest neighbours, the casual friendliness and generosity of the town's inhabitants was seductive. She found herself smiling at everyone she met; calling out greetings from her balcony; even accepting that a ten minute chat about the contents of the sandwich she was ordering was an entirely reasonable use of her time.

And working with Scott continued to enthrall. His knowledge was as inexhaustible as his energy and enthusiasm; and although he was high on ideas he was also entirely open to criticism in a way that made any debate enjoyable, and which invariably brought out the best in both of them.

Often they would discover they had worked straight through their lunch break and that it was mid afternoon before hunger pangs got the better of them. Then, still talking, they would make for the nearest bar and order up a salad and a plate of fries before taking a golf cart out to the surrounding countryside to look at a nesting site. Or they might jump into Scott's boat and visit the nature reserve. Often they didn't return until long after Beth had closed the office and gone home, and even then there would be something else Scott wanted to show her, or a report they needed to discuss. Nor was there any discernable down time. Scott seemed to spend every waking hour working, which drove Claire to do the same.

Eventually Beth put her foot down. "This is getting ridiculous. Shut down your computer and clear your desk. You're coming home to supper with me before this man takes over your life," she told Claire at the end of her second seven-day week.

Aware that she hadn't followed up Beth's invitation to visit the print shop so that she could meet Carl, Claire looked guilty.

Reading her mind, Beth grinned. "You can't avoid him forever you know. Besides, if I don't get you out of here while Scott is on the phone, he'll keep you late again. You're going to have to put your foot down. He's a real slave driver given half a chance."

"I heard that!" Scott reappeared from the inner office with a contrite grin. "I know she's right too. I'm sorry, but I don't do clock watching Claire. I don't even do weekends but it doesn't mean you shouldn't. Besides, you've already proved you're not afraid of hard work, that you'll put in the hours, so if you want to go somewhere, take a day off, come in late, leave early, just do it."

"In that case she can start now. Supper is at six-thirty Claire. You can't miss us because we live over the print shop, which is the last building on Main Street." Beth gathered up her belongings and made for the exit. When she reached the doorway she paused, and then turned and glared at Scott.

"I suppose you'd better come too, but only if you promise not to talk about work!"

Scott waved at her retreating back. "Deal!" he shouted.

Then he turned to Claire. "Carl is a fantastic cook, so never, ever, turn down an invitation to eat with him and Beth."

"I haven't met him yet," Claire told him. "I keep meaning to call into the print shop to be introduced but somehow I haven't gotten around to it."

"Carl's a nice guy. He's a bit quirky but good fun. Beth too, but you already know that."

Claire nodded, her eyes drifting back to the report she was studying, so she wasn't looking at Scott as he added a final snippet of information.

"Beats me why he and Daniel are such good buddies though, considering Daniel and Beth were an item until Carl came onto the scene."

Her head snapped up. "You mean she and Daniel were engaged?"

"As good as, but things changed pretty quickly when Carl came back to Dolphin Key."

Suddenly everything became clear to Claire. Daniel didn't want to date anyone because he was still recovering from being thrown over by his girlfriend...fiancée...Beth! And Carl was feeling so guilty about it that he was doing everything possible to find someone else for his brother. Her heart sank as she realized her chances of ever attracting Daniel had rapidly sunk to zero because there wasn't a chance he would get over his feelings for Beth unless he stopped working with her, and that wasn't going to happen any time soon.

She forced a casual reply. "What was Carl doing while he was away?"

Scott suddenly looked uncomfortable. "I'm sorry Claire, I've been talking out of turn. Forget I said anything. If Beth wants you to know their story she'll tell you."

Claire stared at him. Then she shrugged and returned to her report. As far as Scott was concerned she had lost interest in their conversation and was now completely absorbed in reading about the feeding habits of the dolphins populating the bay. Not by a muscle did she show how much his words had affected her.

Five minutes later she turned off her computer, piled all her paperwork onto one corner of her desk and stood up. She had control of herself now.

"There are a few things I need to do before the stores close, and I'd like to take a quick shower too, so I'll meet you at Beth's."

Scott was so deep into his own work he barely grunted an acknowledgement as she left the office.

* * *

Determined not to think about Daniel at all, Claire walked briskly down Main Street until she reached the bookstore. Despite Beth's warning she had already braved the interior and found that although Tom Cook, the proprietor, lived up to his talkative reputation, he was a nice man. And once she had got past the obligatory conversation and told him what she wanted, he had proved to be both interested and resourceful.

As the large and jangly bell over the door announced her arrival he popped up from behind a pile of books. A small man with a shiny, domed forehead and a neat spade beard, he looked like an oversized garden gnome. He beamed at her, and then disappeared behind the counter again, only to reappear a moment later flourishing a hardback book with a glossy cover.

"I believe this is what you wanted."

Taking it from him, Claire glanced at the cover and smiled. "I hope the illustration looks far more racy than the contents actually are!"

With a laugh he retrieved it and slipped it into a paper bag. "I took the liberty of flicking through it when it first arrived and I can assure you there is nothing exciting in it at all. In fact I'll be surprised if you actually manage to read it aloud to Mr Marchant without falling asleep."

"I'm not even sure he'll let me read it at all yet," she told him as she paid for the book. "But I'm going to try. It's my first move towards persuading him to start using the Talking Books Service."

"I can't imagine why you are going to so much trouble but I'm very pleased you are. Once upon a time Gordon Marchant was one of my best customers; in fact he was close to being a friend, and I enjoyed many a literary debate with him. Then there was all that trouble with Carl, which happened at around the same time his eyes began to let him down. The combination was too much for him. He became so bad tempered that by the time he eventually stopped working he had alienated most of his friends and all his employees."

Uncomfortable talking about her employer's family, even though Tom Cook obviously knew them well, Claire thanked him for getting the book she had ordered, made her excuses and left. As she hurried back to her apartment for a quick shower she wondered about Carl, however. First Scott and now Tom Cook had made allusions to family problems. What had he done that had caused so much trouble? Was it stealing Beth away from Daniel, or was it something else, something that had happened when he was away from Dolphin Key?

Chapter Thirteen

She arrived at the print shop at the same time as Scott. He opened the side door with a familiarity that suggested he was a regular visitor and, calling out to Beth and Carl, led her up a flight of stairs and into an open plan room with hardly any furniture. Instead of chairs there were huge squashy cushions. Smaller cushions were piled onto the one couch as well. Jugs of dried flowers and sea grass, and collections of shells and large pebbles decorated the windowsills and shelves, while watercolors of all shapes and sizes covered the walls.

"So Claire," the man who crossed the room to shake her hand gave her a wry smile. He was as tall as Daniel but very thin, with the dark hair and the sharp features of his father. Where Daniel's nose was short and straight, Carl's was aquiline. And although their eyes were the same warm brown, his were deep set under frowning black brows, while Daniel's were wide apart with long, gold tipped lashes. The smile was the same though, and so was the cleft in his chin. She took his proffered hand, at the same time handing him the bottle of wine she had brought with her.

"Hello Carl!"

It was the closest they would ever get to acknowledging the date he had tried to set up between her and Daniel.

* * *

The evening was one of the best Claire could remember enjoying in a very long time. Not only did the food live up to Scott's promise but Carl and Beth were such thoughtful and entertaining hosts that by the time the meal was over, Claire felt more at ease than she would have believed possible.

Conversation had meandered across so many topics her head was spinning. She learned that Scott had graduated in marine biology and then studied coastal ecosystems, that Beth had come to Dolphin Key to paint and was the source of all the beautiful watercolors adorning the walls of the small apartment, and that Carl, amongst other things, was a talented musician. She also noticed that although he poured the wine she had brought into glasses for her and Scott, he filled his own glass with water. Beth drank water too, but as she was pregnant her abstinence was understandable.

Later, replete, and totally seduced by the lifestyle of her new friends, Claire leaned back amongst the cushions and listened dreamily as Carl strummed his guitar. Maybe she, too, could learn to live like this instead of using books as her window on the world. Maybe she could live the dreams her parents had tried to instill in her after all.

She was laughing at something Scott had said, and had half turned towards him on the cushions when Daniel climbed the stairs, calling out as he did so.

He stopped short on the top step and drank in the scene before him. Lit by a dozen flickering candles, the room was a mix of deep colour and deeper shadow. And the sound of the sea through the open windows was an added enchantment, a backdrop to the soft notes of his brother's guitar. He felt himself relax for the first time in days until his eyes adjusted to the light and he saw who Carl and Beth's visitors were. At the sight of Claire, relaxed and smiling, her head resting against a scarlet cushion next to Scott, her eyes pools of darkness in the dim light, he tensed right up again. He was too late. It was obvious that Scott had beaten him to it.

"This looks like a pretty good gig!" He was surprised at how normal his voice sounded when he spoke.

"Hey Dan! When did you get back?" Carl abandoned his guitar and got to his feet. Although he only touched Daniel's shoulder, Claire saw the affection in his gesture and wondered even more about the mysteries surrounding the Marchant family. Then her eyes met Daniel's and she stopped wondering about his family and started worrying about him.

He looked dreadful. He was tired and drawn, and there was a tracery of fine lines about his eyes that she was sure hadn't been there when she last saw him. Beth appeared to notice the same thing because she quickly went into the kitchen and reappeared with a can of beer and a beef sandwich.

"Sorry, you're too late for the good stuff," she told him as she handed him the plate.

He smiled his thanks as he sank down onto the couch. Carl sat next to him and asked about his trip. Soon the two of them were deep in conversation about the Marchant property development business. Beth gave them a look of disgust as she took up the threads of the conversation that Daniel's arrival had interrupted.

"Ignore them Claire. They have no manners. Tell us more about your work as a librarian. I want to know more about the stuff you did with children."

Doing her best not to eavesdrop on the two men sitting across from her, Claire tried to oblige. She told Beth and Scott about the schools' programme she had introduced, and about the very popular weekly story time for toddlers. She described some of the special events and the competitions she had organised, and then answered the questions they threw at her. At any other time she would have been enthusiastic because she was excited about this part of her job, knowing how important it was for the company to reach out to children and teenagers and teach them all about conservation. Up until now she had been glad she had all the experience needed to get an educational programme up and running. Up until now it had been one of her main enthusiasms, the thing that had her bouncing out of bed before sun up, the thing that stayed in her mind throughout the day even when she was busy doing something else.

She couldn't maintain her enthusiasm now, however. Daniel's proximity, his weary face, the fact he had only looked at her once when he first arrived and had more or less ignored her after that, was all proving too much for her. Needing an escape she glanced at her watch and was relieved to see it was late enough for her to leave without appearing rude. She sat forward on her cushion.

"Beth, it's been a lovely evening but now I'm totally bushed and bed is calling."

"Me too," Scott got to his feet and reached out his hand to pull her up.

Daniel, who despite all outward appearances, had been acutely aware of Claire the whole time he had been talking to Carl, rose to his feet at the same time.

"Please don't go on my account. I'm sorry I intruded on your peaceful evening but I had to discuss a few things with Carl before tomorrow."

"Don't worry. We need to call it a day anyway because we've got an early start tomorrow. I'm going to introduce Claire to the

Suwannee." Scott spoke for both of them as he handed Claire her sweater.

Daniel, who had had every intention of showing Claire the wide sweep of the Suwannee River himself, preferably from a small boat and with a picnic for two, quashed the protest that leapt to his throat. Instead he smiled, and in the soft candlelight it looked like a genuine smile.

"Lucky you. Enjoy yourselves."

"Oh we will, be sure of that!" Scott grinned at him, hugged Beth, slapped Carl on the shoulder and then stood back for Claire to precede him down the stairs.

She managed to thank Beth and Carl for a lovely evening, promise to invite them to a meal at her own apartment as soon as Scott gave her the time to properly settle in, agree that she was looking forward to seeing the Suwannee River, and wish them goodnight, without once giving away her real feelings. Her eyes, when they met Daniel's, conveyed nothing more than a polite friendliness. Then she was gone, down the stairs and outside.

Only Scott, following slowly behind her, frowned. He had been sitting close enough to her to see the sudden tension in her face when Daniel first arrived. And because it was so uncharacteristic, he had been surprised too, by her faltering enthusiasm when she talked about the youth programme they wanted to introduce. Then he had he noticed how often she flicked the tiniest glance across to where Daniel sat talking to Carl and he suddenly wondered if there was more going on than he realized. After all she had moved continents to come to Dolphin Key, and Daniel had pulled out all the stops to make it possible. Now he came to think about it, Daniel's behaviour had been a bit over the top for a new employee. He had organised her work permit and visa, arranged for her to stay in one of his best apartments and then had driven to the airport to meet her himself despite his huge workload. And although she was good it was not even as if her skills were so exceptional that he couldn't have found someone similar in Florida. Maybe if he asked her about her interview with Daniel everything would become clear. It was not until they reached the sidewalk and he saw the frozen expression on her face that he decided not to. After all it was nothing to do with him. He didn't pay the wages. Besides, he had enough emotional problems of his own to deal with; problems that he usually buried in work. And judging by Claire's performance so far, that was exactly what she was doing as well.

* * *

Daniel, meanwhile, was having trouble concentrating on what his brother was saying. It didn't have anything to do with the subject matter either. Instead it had everything to do with Beth's throwaway remark as she walked through to the small kitchen to make more coffee.

"Well that looks like a marriage made in heaven," she said. "Same interests, same stunning looks, same enthusiasms. Looks like Claire's going to be a real asset to the organisation in more ways than one."

* * *

Later, on his solitary journey home, while Claire was lying sleepless in bed, Daniel reflected bitterly on his sister-in-law's words. Was Scott really making a play for Claire, and if he was, was he serious, or was he just indulging in one of his occasional flirtations? The thought made him want to punch something, hard. It was bad enough that the Marchant family's increasingly complicated property portfolio meant that he had to leave Scott running his conservation business more or less singlehanded. If, while he was away, Scott also took over Claire on no more than a whim, then life was going to become even more unbearable.

Chapter Fourteen

After a further ten days of hotel rooms and tedious meetings Daniel finally returned to Dolphin Key, knowing that, for the time being at least, he had saved the family business from yet another crisis. As he drove off the freeway and pointed his car towards the ocean, all he wanted to do was to change into shorts and a T-shirt and take his boat out to the islands, but he knew if he did that then he would only be putting off the moment when he had to talk to his father. With a sigh he turned towards his parent's house. Best to get it over with so he could enjoy the weekend.

He pulled into the driveway and parked next to a golf cart bearing the company logo. He stared at it in surprise. It couldn't be Beth because she never visited, while Scott only ever dropped by if Daniel's sisters were home from college, something that wouldn't be happening again until the summer recess. Then a new thought struck him and, slamming the car door behind him, he hurried towards the house. Maybe something was wrong, something that had forced Beth and his father to drop their mutual antipathy. Maybe his mother was ill.

Her found her in the laundry room. She was standing at the deep sink trimming each stalk of a mass of white flowers before placing them one by one into a large crystal vase. Relieved, he watched her from the doorway, noticing how she carefully positioned each one and then stood back to admire the effect. He noticed, too, that she was smiling, and that there was a hint of colour in her cheeks. He felt his heart lift just a little. At least that was one less problem to deal with.

"They look beautiful," he said as she pushed the final stem into place. And they did because she had always been able to create wonderful floral displays. Until a few years ago she had taken enormous pride in her skills as a flower arranger. She had loved being responsible for the Flower Rota at the local church and for many years had organized the other members into a disciplined team that provided displays for fundraisers, weddings and celebration dinners; anything that needed flowers.

Sadly it had all stopped when his father had started to lose his sight and demanded she stay at home to be his eyes, which was why the sight of her smiling over a vase of beautifully arranged flowers had such an uplifting effect on his spirits. It was like a whisper from a happier past.

She gave a sudden start when she heard his voice, but when she turned and looked at him, the smile was still in place. "Goodness, you startled me Daniel. I didn't hear you come in. Yes, they do look beautiful don't they? And she was so clever to include some greenery, especially the sprays of ivy. Without them it would just be a vase of flowers, not a lovely display."

"Um…yes, I suppose so," Daniel was completely indifferent to the niceties of floral decoration.

To his amazement his mother laughed at him as she cleared away the trimmed stems and the sheets of cellophane the flowers had been wrapped in. "I know I'm boring you, so don't try to look interested. Would you carry them through to the dining room for me though? They will look wonderful against the dark wood of the table."

Picking up the vase he followed her through the kitchen to the formal dining room and placed the display exactly where she told him. Then he waited patiently while she adjusted several of the blooms and tweaked a couple of leaves before asking her if Beth had bought them.

She turned towards him with wide, puzzled eyes. "Beth? No of course not! You know she won't come here. It was Claire. She's in the study reading to your Father."

* * *

Now it was Daniel's turn to look wide-eyed and, unexpectedly, his mother laughed again when she saw the expression on his face.

"Apparently she found a copy of some dry-as-dust biography he mentioned when you first brought her to see us, and she dropped it in last week. He was so pleased when she suggested she read it to him. Apparently it's beyond my intellectual capacity...your Father's words, not Claire's!"

She appeared to be amused rather than offended by her husband's judgment, or was it relief? Was she relieved that an irksome duty had, for the time being at least, been taken away from her. Daniel stared at her, unable to believe the change that Claire appeared to have wrought in both of his parents while he was away.

"She's staying for supper," his mother added. "Up until now she's refused but the last time she came I insisted, hence the flowers."

"You mean she's been before?"

"Oh yes. She reads to him most evenings. She usually only stays for an hour or so but we've both begun to look forward to her visit. That's why I persuaded her to stay for supper tonight. Do you want to join us or are you anxious to get home? I know you've had a busy week."

Suddenly Daniel's gray business suit was no longer a hot and irksome restriction. "I'll stay," he said, stripping off his jacket and tie and throwing them over the nearest chair.

"Good. In that case you can carry a jug of lemonade out onto the deck. I made it earlier with crushed ice, so it will be lovely and cold. I'm sure Claire's throat must have seized up by now. I'll go and tell her it's time she stopped reading."

As she opened the door into the main part of the house, Daniel heard the soft cadences of Claire's voice for the first time. He couldn't hear the words but the intonation was clear. She was reading something that was amusing and his father was chuckling. He looked at his mother. She had heard it too and as the chuckles turned to a full-throated laugh, she met Daniels gaze. Her face was ineffably sad.

"I wish I could do that! But I can't. I've tried."

"I know you have," he gave her a quick hug. "We all have, but maybe we're just too close to the problem."

"What do you mean?"

"Well Claire doesn't have any sort of emotional attachment does she? And she loves books too. So maybe she is exactly what he needs; someone who doesn't remember him as he used to be; someone who likes him for himself and just wants to help."

"You could be right," she nodded doubtfully. "She's even made him promise to think about trialing the Talking Books Service."

Shaking his head in disbelief, Daniel picked up a tray laden with a full jug of lemonade, frosted glasses and a dish of pecans, and carried

156

it out onto the deck, leaving his mother to interrupt the reading session.

* * *

Claire, who had thought that Daniel was going to be away from Dolphin Key for at least one more day, flushed pink when she saw him leaning against the railings that edged the deck, a glass of lemonade in one hand and a scoop of pecans in the other. Fortunately for her, however, the sunset had already tinted everything with a matching glow, so her confusion went unnoticed as he tipped the last of the nuts down his throat before leaning forward and handing her a glass of lemonade.

She took a sip, and then pulled her sunglasses down onto her nose from the top of her head. She had pushed them up there while she was reading but now she was glad that the sunset gave her an excuse to cover her eyes.

"Hi Dad. Seems that a few things have changed around here while I've been away," Daniel directed his comment to his father with a smile, while his own eyes, similarly hidden behind sunglasses, watched Claire. Dressed in a pale green sundress, and tinted with the rosy glow of the setting sun, she was even more beautiful than he remembered. His body reacted accordingly, pushing his blood pressure up to what felt like a danger zone.

His father's reply was short and to the point. "She likes books."

"Hmm. Even your dry and dusty ones?"

"Even those! Now tell me about your trip. Did you achieve everything I wanted?"

"I did but I'll talk to you about it later. Right at this moment I think you should concentrate on entertaining your guest. After all she's put in a full day's work and then come straight over to read to you, so it's the least you can do."

There was a long silence as a number of expressions, each one blacker than the last, washed across Gordon Marchant's face. Then it cleared and he nodded.

"You're right of course. Sorry young lady. My manners seem to have gotten a little rusty. I haven't even asked you about your day."

Mrs Marchant, whose face had frozen with horror at Daniel's words, let out a sigh of relief. "Supper in thirty minutes," she told them as she hurried off to set the table and prepare the last minute vegetables.

* * *

The evening was a success on all counts. For the first time since he lost his sight Gordon Marchant concentrated on being a good host, even insisting on choosing the wine to go with the meal. Gone was his previous indifference to what was going on around him. Instead, he complimented his wife on the food, asked Claire about her family and her previous job, talked to Daniel about the boat he was renovating, and was altogether congenial if slightly acerbic company. This had the effect of putting the sparkle back into his wife's eyes, and by the time dessert was served she had relaxed enough to reminisce about the past when her family was young, and when her husband was making his way in the world.

Claire heard about the hard times when they had to scrimp and scrape to save enough money for a down payment on their first property. She heard too about their eventual success and how, when they first moved to Dolphin Bay, Daniel had often been in trouble for cutting school to row out to the islands long before they became a nature reserve.

The telling was affectionate enough, as were the tales about Daniel's older sister who now lived in Texas with her husband and two small children, and his younger twin sisters who were still at college. Yet through it all Claire could detect a note of censure, a reproof, a feeling that they didn't think any of their children had quite lived up to the standards set for them, that none of them would ever be able to achieve what their father had.

She also noticed that they never mentioned Carl. Not even once. He didn't feature in any of the conversations, nor did Beth; so by the time she was ready to leave she was as intrigued about the complicated family dynamics as she was about the other thing that had become clear during the evening; Daniel's obvious reluctance to talk to his parents about his own company.

Of more importance, however, was what sitting opposite Daniel was doing to her. Every time his long brown eyes met her gray ones her pulse sped up, and when he leaned across to top up her wine glass, or hand her a plate, or hold a serving dish for her, she felt as if every vein and artery in her body had heated up by several degrees. Worried that he would see how she felt if she looked at him for too long, she spent most of the evening avoiding his gaze and concentrating on his parents instead.

Frustrated by her behaviour, Daniel wondered if it had anything to do with Scott. If they *were* involved with one another, then maybe she was embarrassed. He remembered the vehemence with which she had told him she wasn't looking for any sort of date and decided she was probably feeling uncomfortable about how quickly she had changed her mind. Whatever the reason, he needed to know how things stood. He needed to know whether he had any sort of chance with her. With this in mind he rose to his feet when she stood up to leave.

"I thought we were going to talk business," his father said sharply when Daniel wished him goodnight.

"Tomorrow Dad," he told him wearily. "I'm going to see Claire home now. I'll come back early tomorrow morning."

"Make sure you do!" Gordon Marchant's habitual irascibility had risen to the surface again.

Daniel ignored him, kissed his mother's cheek, and held open the door for Claire. She thanked her host and hostess, promised to return the following week to continue reading to Mr Marchant, and then walked past Daniel into the magnificent, high-beamed hallway that was full of decorative plants and highly polished wooden furniture. He followed her, inhaling her perfume until he was intoxicated by it, and by the way her hips swayed as she walked in front of him.

When they stepped onto the gravel driveway she turned and faced him with a determined look on her face.

"I can manage to get home by myself," she said. "I don't think much is going to happen to me in Dolphin Key at this time of night, do you? I've already studied the town's crime statistics and they are virtually nil. Besides, you would look ridiculous following me in your car at golf cart speed."

"I guess I'd look a lot like a stalker," he admitted with a rueful grin. "Sorry Claire. I forgot you had your golf cart parked outside."

Mollified, she grinned back at him. She could manage Daniel when they were surrounded by darkness and his eyes were nothing but black shadows. It was looking at him in daylight that did for her.

"How was your week anyway? Did you manage to achieve everything you wanted to?"

He nodded, frustrated by the formality of their conversation even while he acknowledged to himself that it was better than nothing. "Yes thanks. You too?"

"More or less. Every time I think I'm getting the hang of it, Scott comes up with something else, but we're beginning to formulate some good plans for the future. We'll tell you all about them next week, that's assuming that you'll have time to come into the office."

"I will." Hearing the warmth in her voice as she referred to Scott he decided that he wasn't up to questioning her about their relationship after all. He would know how they felt about one another when he saw them together again. Besides, what could he actually say? *Are you and Scott and item* wasn't the normal sort of conversation an employer had with a member of his staff. She would be quite within her rights to tell him to mind his own business.

"I guess it's goodnight then," he began to turn away, then a thought that had been niggling at him all evening struck him, and he turned back. He needed to understand why she was prepared to spend so much of her time with his father when she was getting nothing for her pains except an occasional grudging thank you, a thank you that was probably counterbalanced by a lot of personal criticism when her pronunciation or reading style didn't suit.

His question died on his lips, however, when he saw the expression of desolation that filled her face. It was so stark and unexpected that it tripped his tongue. For a moment he

162

could only stand and look at her and wonder what had prompted it. Then, seconds later, when she gave him an odd little smile and began to speak, he wondered if he had imagined it after all.

"Daniel, I hope...that is I don't want to seem inquisitive...but what is the problem between Carl and your parents?" her voice was tentative. "His name wasn't mentioned once this evening. Scott and Beth have both alluded to difficulties too, although without explaining anything. So did Tom Cook at the bookshop, so I know it's not a secret. I'm sorry to ask but...well, it's just that I don't want to be put in the position where I might say something out of turn," she added by way of explanation when he didn't immediately reply.

"You're right to ask. I guess none of us mentioning his name this evening was a bit of a giveaway," he sighed. "I'm sorry Claire. I would have told you earlier if I had known you were going to get so involved with my family."

She looked embarrassed. "I hope you don't mind that I've become friendly with them. It...just...sort of happened. It's the librarian in me I'm afraid. I thought that if I could persuade your father to start using the Talking Books Service it would...well it would help your mother. He doesn't exactly try to make himself any less of a burden to her does he?"

He gave a bitter laugh. "You can say that again! And no, of course I don't mind how often you visit them. I just don't understand why you would want to give up so much of your time for nightly readings to a grumpy, embittered old man."

"Oh that! That's just a means to an end," she told him with the flash of the humour he so loved to see. "I'm not going to do it forever. It's the first stage of introducing him to Talking Books. I know how good it is, and how much it would help him to feel less isolated. He just needs persuading."

He gave a slow nod. "Well I hope you're right because I don't think my mother can cope with things as they are much longer."

Her smile became warmer as she reached out and briefly touched his arm. It was only a placatory pat but to Daniel it was as if a thousand volts had shot through his body. "Don't worry. I know what I'm doing. And Tom Cook is on my side too."

Trying to ignore the effect her touch had had on him, he stared at her, and then he laughed out loud. "That incorrigible old rascal! He was one of Dad's best friends once upon a time but I thought he had abandoned him, like everyone else."

"Nobody has abandoned him," she told him. "It's just that he won't talk to anyone anymore. It's fairly normal, this grieving for what he once had you know."

"Is that what he's doing?"

"Yes. Any physical loss can affect people badly. It can plunge them into depression and despair although fortunately most of them recover in time."

"And you're determined my father will too."

She nodded, and then returned to her earlier question. "About Carl. I wish you'd tell me what has happened between him and your father. I don't want to say the wrong thing and inadvertently undo everything I've achieved so far."

He nodded as he made a decision. "That makes sense but let's not talk about it here. It's still early so how about you come back to my place for coffee? We can sit out on the dock and talk about it there without any danger of being overheard. Besides I would like to hear more about your week too. After all I did abandon you less than halfway through showing you the ropes."

She took a deep breath as she also made her own decision. "Okay. But tell me where you live so you don't have to drive along at four miles an hour while I follow you."

"I can do better than that. Go home and park your buggy and I'll follow on in a few minutes and drive you back to mine. It's a bit far out for you to trundle back home on your own late at night."

Chapter Fifteen

By the time Daniel arrived to pick her up from outside her apartment Claire was in a state of panic. Whatever had made her agree to spend another hour or so with him, and at his house too? When he drew up beside her and leaned across to unlock the passenger door, she leaned in through the open window to speak to him.

"Are you sure you want to do this now? You must be tired after your busy week."

"I'm sure," he told her. "Besides you already know how jet lag affects me, so you'll be doing me a favour...again!"

With no way out she climbed into the car. He turned it around and drove back down Main Street until he hit the coastal road and then kept going for several more minutes. When he stopped there wasn't a street lamp in sight. Instead, his house was lit up by the moonlight that reflected off its walls and windows, and danced across the white boat tied up to the dock.

"Wow! And I thought I had a wonderful view," Claire climbed out of the car and looked around her. His house was actually on the beach, tucked into a hidden cove well away from the places used by visiting tourists.

166

"Unfortunately I don't get to see enough of it," Daniel led the way around to the back of the house and unlocked the folding glass doors that opened out onto the dock.

Claire followed him inside and propped herself against the kitchen counter while he spooned instant coffee into two mugs.

"I'm sorry but I'm out of milk," he told her as he opened the refrigerator. "In fact I seem to be out of everything," he added, peering into an empty cookie barrel on the counter. "It's one of the many downsides of being away so much."

"Without milk is fine by me," Claire picked up her mug and carried it outside. She didn't want to stay in his house any more. It was too full of Daniel, too redolent of everything she found attractive about him. Casually furnished but with a comfortable couch and a rocking chair, it had shelves of books, and sturdy pegs on which all-weather gear jostled with baseball caps and backpacks. A jumble of walking boots and trainers were stored in a wooden box beside the door alongside a coil of rope, several oars and, surreally, a rusty anchor. It was masculine but welcoming, painted white, but somehow full of warmth.

After a few false starts she had finally learned that the suited and booted Daniel who followed her outside wasn't the real Daniel. The real Daniel was someone who was more at home in a boat, or with binoculars swinging from his neck as he strode across fields or through woodland, and his home exactly illustrated that, which was why she had to be outside, her face unreadable in the shadows of the evening.

Daniel joined her, and for a few moments they sat in silence on the edge of the dock, their feet barely skimming the water. Then he began to talk about Carl.

"It all began when he had to start thinking about college," he said. "Up until then he was just a normal kid. He wasn't even very rebellious, mainly because he liked learning while I was always looking for ways to escape the classroom and make for the beach."

He stared out across the bay as he spoke and because he wasn't looking at her Claire was able to study his face in the moonlight. She saw how tired the past few weeks of travelling had made him; how too much time driving or sitting in a plane and too much time spent in long and difficult meetings, had leached the suntan from his face. She saw, too, how his hair needed trimming, how it was beginning to grow into a tangle of waves instead of its usual neatly groomed shape, waves that she wanted to run her fingers through. With a sharp intake of breath she sat on her hands and forced herself to concentrate on what he was saying.

"I guess he was...is my best friend. There's less than two years between us, so although we are very different we always spent a lot of time together as kids. When I went off to college though, months could go by without us talking to each other, so I didn't know there was a problem until it was too late."

He turned and looked at Claire, his expression unexpectedly fierce as it was disturbed by bad memories. "You see he loves music and he's good at it. His guitar was always his most prized possession. He never went anywhere without it until Dad decided that his obsession was stopping him from getting good grades in his senior year, and locked it away in his study. Apparently there was a ferocious shouting match, but then Carl just seemed to give up and accept it; except he didn't of course. If only I'd been at home I would have realized and perhaps been able to stop what happened next…"

"Which was…?" Claire was too immersed in the story to remember that being close to Daniel was dangerous, so she didn't drag her eyes away from his. Instead she stared straight at him as she waited for him to continue.

"He spent a few weeks making plans and then he cracked open the cupboard in the study one evening when my parents were attending some sort of fundraiser and reclaimed his guitar. Then he threw a few clothes into a backpack along with every penny he had saved from working weekends at the local store, and disappeared.

"It took us years to find him because he stayed on the move, living in squats and dosshouses while he put a band together, and always playing under a different name. Mother

169

was beside herself with worry of course, but Dad was too full of fury to care. He wouldn't take any of the blame for what had happened. He couldn't see that he had brought it all on himself. As far as he was concerned Carl was just feckless and lazy."

"But surely Carl contacted you so you wouldn't worry?"

Daniel nodded. "Yes, a few times, just to let me know he was okay; but only by postcard, and never from the same place twice."

"And that's it? That's why your father still refuses to speak to him, just because he did something stupid when he was a kid?"

"If only it were that simple but there's more. You see after a while Carl became successful and with his success came money, quite a lot of money, enough to get him hooked on the highlife. There were three-day parties, too many girls, and too much booze... I guess you can fill the rest of it in for yourself."

Daniel paused for so long as the memories of the past flooded through him that in the end Claire was again forced to ask him what had happened.

"Eventually, after years, I received a phone call from one of his friends saying Carl was ill. He gave me an address where I could find him. It was in a city on the other side of the country. I caught the next plane out without telling anyone where I was going. I didn't want to do anything that might jeopardize some sort of family rapprochement.

"Unfortunately it was too late. The Carl I found was a different person from the boy who had left home. He was a bitter man, thin and emaciated, and suffering in every possible way from the effects of a hedonistic life on the road. He was pleased to see me though, and right then that was enough.

"I took him to a doctor who told him in no uncertain terms that he was killing himself. He said if he didn't get out into the country, eat good food, fill his lungs with fresh air, and take stock of his life, he'd be dead within a year. Carl was too weak to do any of that on his own though, so I brought him home. He protested all the way but really he didn't have a choice."

"And when you got here you introduced him to Beth," the words were out before Claire could stop herself. She winced and hoped he wouldn't notice that she already knew about his own relationship with Beth.

"No, not right away. To start with he wouldn't meet anyone. He begged me not to tell anyone he was back in Dolphin Key, especially our parents. He just sort of huddled in a chair on my porch and stared out into the bay. And he couldn't get warm. I used to pile covers on him and leave hot soup and coffee in a couple of flasks when I went to work. Then, when I returned home, I would try to feed him something nourishing. Really he needed Mum but he was adamant about not telling anyone he was home. In the end I insisted I tell Beth because she was my girlfriend then, and she was getting fed up with the fact that I kept going home early every evening without inviting her along."

His reference to Beth was so casual that for a moment Claire could almost believe that losing her to Carl meant nothing to him. He soon disabused her of the thought, however.

"In the end she insisted on visiting of course. She was all set to give him a piece of her mind for being so difficult. She said I had done enough for him and it was about time he took some responsibility for himself. That was before she met him though. When she actually saw him...well even I could see I was going to be fighting a lost cause if I tried to come between them. As far as Beth was concerned, I no longer existed!"

Claire heard the wry humor in his voice and identified with the pain he was trying to hide. She had been like that when she had been thrown over for someone else all those years ago. She had joked about it and pretended it didn't matter in the daytime, and then had cried herself to sleep at night.

"Meeting her was his turning point though," Daniel continued. "She gave him back his love of life, and soon he was strong enough to walk into town. Then Beth told him it was time he visited our parents."

"They must have been pleased to have him back in one piece, surely."

"My mother was. I'll never forget the expression on her face the day I told her he had come home."

"But your father wouldn't forgive him?"

"You've got it in one! If he wouldn't forgive him when he first left, then he certainly wasn't about to forgive a son who he regarded a drunken, dope-addled hippy, a son who had come home with his tail between his legs. That was *his* interpretation, of course, and it was very far from the truth.

"I tried to explain it wasn't like that at all. That Carl had been ill not drunk, and that he was recovering fast. Then I suggested we offer him a job in the family business to help him get back on his feet."

"And it didn't go down well!"

"It certainly did not. For a moment I thought he was going to throw me out of the house too."

He turned and looked at her. "So now you have it, the entire unedifying Marchant family saga. Nowadays there are a few upsides of course, such as Carl and Beth getting married and starting a family and the fact that Carl now runs his own successful print business, but Dad still won't talk to him."

"And your poor mother is in the middle of it all," Claire's heart went out to Mrs Marchant. No wonder the poor woman looked so strained and sad when she had a son she wasn't allowed to mention, let alone see, and a husband who demanded she look after him every hour of the day and night.

"Mmm. Well she's sort of found a way around that. She calls into the print shop for coffee whenever she manages to get into town. And occasionally I shut myself into the study with Dad for what he thinks is a business meeting, and make it last long enough for her to have lunch with Carl and Beth as well."

* * *

Suddenly Daniel was bored with his family history. It was something he didn't like to dwell on, and he had only told Claire because she needed to know. If she hadn't taken to visiting his parents and reading to his father then it would have been a very long time before she found out the truth about the Marchant family. He stood up.

"I'll pour some more coffee and then we'll talk about something far more interesting, your week for example."

He didn't wait for her answer and Claire frowned as she watched him retreat into the house carrying their empty mugs. Life in Dolphin Key wasn't as uncomplicated and serene as it appeared to be after all. Underneath its smiling face were the dark undercurrents of family feuds and broken relationships. She thought of her own parents with a sudden surge of affection because she knew it would never ever occur to either of them to stop her doing something she loved. Nor would they ever disown her, or refuse to speak to her, whatever she did.

For the first time in her life she stopped dwelling on the difficulties of her unorthodox childhood and began to appreciate what they *had* given her instead. Their loving but hands-off parenting had given her the freedom to develop her own interests without any pressure. Unlike Carl, who had had his music taken away, she had been able to pursue her own obsession with photography with their blessing. Nor had they ever tried to make her into someone that she wasn't. Instead they had merely insisted she stay with them and learn to adjust when their lives changed, rather than shut herself away in the boarding school she had once hankered for. And despite her hang ups, and however difficult she had found it at the time, she had to admit that all the travelling and the new experiences had left her with an inner confidence in her own abilities and a knowledge that she was totally her own person.

She accepted a second mug of coffee with a murmur of thanks, wondering, as she did so, how badly the story Daniel had told her had affected him. She wanted to ask him but she didn't dare. He had already opened a small portion of his heart, and from the troubled expression on his face that was more than enough for one night.

"My week was good," she told him. She was rewarded by a broad smile, and soon they were talking about some of the ideas she and Scott had come up with during the past few days. As they talked Daniel's face gradually relaxed, and he laughed aloud as she recounted her latest success.

"You mean you have actually persuaded Scott to pose for our leaflets as some sort of poster boy!"

"There was no persuasion! She and Beth blackmailed me into it!" Scott's voice, coming out of the surrounding darkness, made them both jump. He joined them on the dock.

"I was driving past when I noticed the lights were on in the house so I knew you were back Dan. I guess it's kind of late for a work update but knowing how you don't sleep when you've been travelling, I thought I'd stop by anyway. Tell me if I'm intruding."

"You're not," Claire and Daniel protested in unison, shifting away from one another as they did so.

"We've been talking work, " Daniel explained. Then he grinned. "As you heard, we were just about to discuss your new role as in-house model!"

Scott, who had noticed their involuntary movement away from each other and heard the unnecessary emphasis in their voices when they told him he wasn't intruding, inwardly cursed himself for stopping by at all. There was something going on here, so why weren't they owning up to it? What was the matter with them? He gave an imperceptible shrug. Best play the game.

"As I said, it was blackmail," he said with a false frown. "Both of them told me I owed it to the company, that if I didn't do it then any shortfall in our visitor numbers would be all my fault."

"He means female visitor numbers," Claire told Daniel with a grin. "He's just too modest to say it!"

Daniel chuckled. "I'm impressed. In less than a month you've managed to turn my ultra macho Operations Manager into a piece of female eye candy!"

"She has not!" Scott growled. "One day is all I'm giving her. One day to take all the photos she wants. After that nobody is allowed to mention it ever again."

Claire and Daniel roared with laughter at his furious scowl, a scowl that grew blacker as Claire spelled out the sort of shots she intended to take, the poses he would have to hold.

"You owe me," he told her when she finished. "You owe me big time Claire Harris and don't think I won't collect!"

Then, unable to keep up a pretense of fury any longer, he joined in with the laughter. And after that the three of them moved indoors where they stayed until late talking about work and the plans they all had for the future of the company. When Scott eventually stood up to leave, thinking that perhaps it was time he left them alone, Claire stood up too.

"Will you give me a lift home?" she asked him.

"Of course," he hid his surprise as he glanced at Daniel, but his friend's face was expressionless as he gathered up the coffee mugs and walked towards the kitchen.

Chapter Sixteen

Scott's photo shoot was the source of a great deal of amusement in Dolphin Key. Word got around and soon he had an audience of fishermen, shopkeepers and bemused tourists while Claire photographed him supposedly clearing undergrowth, building a boardwalk, and setting off for the islands in his dinghy. She even took one photo where he was explaining the finer details of some of the local flora to Beth who, determined to enjoy her own brief publicity, produced a suitably enraptured expression as if she was hanging onto his every word. They were all good macho shots that showed off Scott's physical attributes to perfection while also illustrating the work he was involved in. Once she was satisfied with them, she insisted on taking some softer ones; Scott talking to a group of small children at the local school; a close up of him holding a newly hatched bird that had fallen from its nest, and which he was rearing; and finally, at the end of the day, a picture of him sitting on the beach watching a flock of birds fly across the sunset.

"Those last ones are for the 'ah' factor," she told him with a grin as she packed away her camera. "A girl likes nothing better than to see a macho man reduced to gooeyness!"

Then she ran away shrieking as he chased her across the sand. "Mind my camera Scott," she pleaded when he caught up with her.

He smiled wickedly as he very deliberately removed it from her grasp and put it on the boardwalk while still keeping one arm tightly around her. Then he picked her up, covered the area between the boardwalk and the sea at a run, and dumped her into the sun-warmed water of the bay. She came up spluttering and then, not to be outdone, she started splashing him.

He retreated up the beach. "Mind the camera," he mimicked, and then he doubled over with laughter as she lost her footing and was submerged for a second time. When she resurfaced she was covered in seaweed.

"You asked for it," he told her as he helped her out of the water and picked some of the longer strands out of her hair.

"I guess so," she looked suitably contrite as she pushed her wet hair out of her eyes. Then she dumped a fistful of wet sand down the front of his T-shirt. With a roar of surprise he tried to grab her again but this time she eluded him and ran up the beach to retrieve her camera. When she straightened up she had a sudden sense of déjà vu because a very tall man was standing in front of her.

"Daniel," she exclaimed, wishing her heart wouldn't do that double beat thing every time he appeared. "I thought you were in Miami today."

"I was. I'm back," he told her. "I guess Scott didn't enjoy his modeling debut then."

Ineffectually trying to wring some of the water out of her T-shirt, she shook her head. "You could say that!"

Scott came padding up the beach to join them, a huge grin on his face. "She deserved everything she got. She has done nothing but needle me all day. Professional photographer indeed!"

"I so have not," Claire protested. "I did everything I could to make it easy for you."

Scott knew she had but as a matter of principle he kept on bickering with her as the three of them walked back to the entrance of her apartment block. Daniel, however, didn't say very much at all. He was too busy trying to forget what he had seen as he walked down onto the beach in search of Claire, because the sight of Scott picking strands of seaweed out of her hair with one hand while he pulled her up out of the water with the other had been almost more than he could bear.

It was only when she said goodbye and turned towards her apartment that he finally found his voice. "I came to ask if you would like to come to the State Reserve with me tomorrow. I've got a meeting out there and if you come with me it will give you a chance to get to know some of the rangers. It will be an opportunity for you to see a different type of local habitat as well."

"Yes, of course." Claire wasn't sure why she felt so embarrassed standing in front of him in dripping shorts and a wrung out T-shirt. She couldn't believe that he cared about her and Scott larking about on the beach, especially as it was an hour after the office had closed. Yet there was something deep in his eyes that made her uncomfortable, a look of reproach that didn't make any sort of sense.

"Good. I'll pick you up around nine." His smile didn't quite reach his eyes as he nodded his approval.

Full of confusion, she watched him walk away. She had obviously done something to upset him but she couldn't imagine what it was. Dispiritedly she trailed damp footprints onto the walkway of her apartment block, waving to Scott as she went.

He returned her wave, then looked at Daniel's retreating back and sighed. Whatever was going on between those two was far too complicated for him. He set off along the road at a steady jog. A five-kilometer run would clear his head, something that was needed after the day he had just had. There was no way he intended being a photographer's model ever again.

* * *

By the time Daniel picked Claire up the following morning they had both been up for hours.

Daniel had watched the sun come up as he paddled his dinghy in a desultory fashion around the islands, supposedly checking on nesting sites, but actually thinking about Claire and wondering how he was going to be able to cope with her burgeoning relationship with Scott.

Claire had dealt with her own sleeplessness by watching the sunrise from her balcony and then jogging for a couple of kilometers along the coastal path in the opposite direction from Daniel's hidden cove. By the time she returned to her apartment, hot and red-faced, and turned on her shower, she had solved her dilemma. Commonsense told her that Daniel's uncharacteristic moodiness the previous day was nothing to do with her at all because she was sure she hadn't done anything wrong, so she would just ignore it. And if he behaved in the same way when he arrived this morning, well she would cut him some slack. After all he had a lot to deal with; his parents; his brother; the family business; his own business; even the breakup of his relationship with Beth which, although it was a long time ago, probably still affected him. She knew from her own experience how long it could take to get over heartbreak. She also knew how close she was to heartbreak again but she resolutely turned the shower up to full blast when the thought surfaced. That was something that she wasn't going to think about at all.

* * *

When she climbed into Daniel's car a few minutes past nine o'clock, artful makeup ensured that she looked as fresh as if she had only recently woken from a good night's sleep. Carrying her camera bag, and dressed in cotton chinos, walking boots and a green T-shirt with the company logo on its vest pocket, she was every inch the professional.

"You look keen," Daniel smiled across at her as she strapped herself into the passenger seat, and congratulated himself on how normal he sounded; how the pulse at the base of his throat, the one that had begun beating rapidly as soon as he saw her, didn't seem to be affecting his vocal chords

"I am," Claire nodded, thankful he seemed to have reverted to his old self. "I checked out the State Reserve's website last night and saw that it is home to a lot of wild turkeys. I'd really love to capture some on camera."

He laughed. "There speaks a newcomer. Wild turkeys live all over Florida, Claire. There's nothing very special about them. In fact hunting them is one of our national pastimes. You're right about the Reserve though. You are far more likely to see them there than anywhere else because of the way the rangers manage the habitat."

He gave her a curious look as he started the engine. "You really are into the flora and fauna around here aren't you? I've looked at some of the photos you've taken and they're good. Better than good! Your enthusiasm shines through. What happened to the Claire Harris who so nearly didn't come to Florida?"

"Oh her, she disappeared halfway across the Atlantic when I started reading a book Scott had sent me! The pictures in it were so stunning I suddenly realized I had been in danger of almost throwing away the opportunity of a lifetime," Claire told him with a laugh. "That was the moment when I decided I had better change my attitude and just enjoy it…and yes, you can say 'I told you so,' if you want to."

"It's tempting but I won't," he said. "I'm just pleased you changed your mind and decided to give it a try, although I'm surprised you were half way across the Atlantic before that happened. What got you onto the plane in the first place if you were still so uncertain?"

"Pride!"

"Pride?"

"Yes. Having said I was going to do it, I wasn't prepared to lose face by changing my mind and turning your offer down, although I must admit I came pretty close once or twice. And despite my initial irritation with them, the thought of my parents' disappointment also proved to be a spur. They were so excited by the thought that I was at last going to do something challenging, so pleased I was showing signs of having inherited a little of their adventurous spirit, that changing my mind wasn't really an option."

185

"And there was I thinking it was my charm that had persuaded you," Daniel teased as he filtered onto the highway.

She gave a slight frown as she glanced across at him. "Is that what you call it...persuasion. It seemed more like emotional blackmail at the time."

He returned her gaze with a twinkle in his eyes. "I probably do owe you an apology for my behavior that weekend but I still think the end result justifies the means. You must admit you are made for this job."

"I wouldn't give you the satisfaction!" Claire's attempt at humorous indignation badly backfired as their eyes met, and she was the one to look away moments before he reluctantly turned his attention back to the highway.

Eventually he broke the silence that followed by talking about the forthcoming meeting, the development of the State Reserve, and where they were mostly likely to see the wild turkeys.

"We'll go look for them as soon as this meeting is over," he promised as he pulled into the car park. "Spring has been pretty warm this year so there might have been some early hatchings. If there have been then we might get lucky and see a hen foraging with her poults."

* * *

The meeting took two hours and when it was over someone brought in a huge platter of sandwiches, some bottled water and some juice. Claire, who was feeling ravenous after her early start, tucked in enthusiastically. Now she understood that working partnerships were an integral part of eco management across the State, she had a hundred more questions to ask. Daniel was busy talking to his neighbor so she turned to the man sitting next to her.

"You specialize in bats, right?" she asked him.

He grinned at her. "Bat preservation and conservation sounds better!"

"I guess it does," she laughed. "And if I ever find an orphaned or injured bat then I need to get in touch with you."

"That's about it. Then I put you in touch with a local rescue volunteer who cares for the bat until it's ready to be released back into the wild."

"And everyone around the table represents a different organisation?"

"Yes. There are people here who look after nature trails or who specialize in gopher tortoise preservation. Others organize wildlife research or maybe just represent a particular area that their community thinks should be preserved. There's a place at the table for everyone."

"So it's a sort of conservation network?"

"You could call it that I guess." He grinned at her. "And if you have any more questions I'd be glad to answer them over supper tonight."

"I bet you would, but it's a no go Stan!" Daniel had stopped talking to his neighbor and turned back to Claire just in time to hear her neighbor's proposition. There was a hint of steel in his voice as he answered for her.

"Hey! I was just asking," Stan's voice was apologetic. "I didn't know you two were an item."

"We're not," Claire said, glaring at Daniel as she pushed back her chair. "And it was sweet of you to ask, but I can't tonight I'm afraid. Another time perhaps."

* * *

"What makes you think you can interfere in my private life?" she asked Daniel angrily as soon as they were out of earshot. "I'm quite capable of making my own decisions you know!"

He didn't look in the least contrite. "He's a lech and he knows it. I was just looking out for you."

"Well don't! I already managed to negotiate a lot of bad Internet dates if you remember, so I'm quite capable of recognising a bad proposition when I get one."

"I guess," Daniel seemed about to say something else, but then he shrugged and changed the subject. "I've found out where we'll see the wild turkeys, so how about we duck out of the networking bit and go look for them."

Slightly mollified, Claire agreed. She couldn't begin to imagine what had gotten into him but it was clear he wanted to stop arguing as much as she did, so the sooner they changed the subject the better. Retrieving her camera bag from beneath her chair she smiled apologetically at Stan, waved a general farewell to everyone in the room, and followed Daniel outside.

* * *

"Look! They're over there in that long grass. Can you see the hen's head bobbing up and down?"

Claire and Daniel were crouched down close to one another behind a fallen tree, peering through its network of shriveled branches. In front of them was a grassy clearing surrounded by patches of dense vegetation and a few trees. Claire, her camera ready, hardly dared to breathe as the turkey hen led her brood of poults towards them.

"There are so many of them," she whispered to Daniel in amazement as the last one broke cover.

"Each hen lays anything between ten to twelve eggs," he told her. "Not that many of them make it to hatching. Bobcats, raccoons, skunk, owls, hawks, bald eagles, even snakes, all enjoy turkey eggs. It doesn't get any better after they've hatched either. Only about thirty per cent survive more than a couple of weeks. I would guess that this lot are seven or eight days old."

She stared at him and then returned her gaze to where the foraging poults had suddenly stopped as a group to investigate something in front of them on the ground. "That's terrible!"

He gave a wry smile. "That's nature Claire! The wild turkey is what is known as a prey species, which means almost everything likes to eat it, even humans. That's why the hen lays such a large clutch of eggs. It's the only way the species can survive."

Then he laughed. "Hey look! They've just found a tortoise."

Claire, following the direction of his pointing finger, joined in with his laughter. The poults were darting around what appeared to be a slow moving boulder and making excited cheeping noises. She pointed her camera and took a several pictures, safe in the knowledge that they were making too much noise to hear the faint click each time the shutter closed.

She was still clicking away when suddenly the little family in front of her was torn apart by a dark flurry of beating wings as a hawk swooped down out of nowhere and seized one of the squawking poults in its claws. Instantly the rest of them vanished and Claire was left staring at an empty space.

"That was awful," she said shakily, lowering her camera. "I mean I know it's nature and all that but...well it was still awful to see it happen so close up."

"It wasn't nice but you get used to it when you work with nature every day," Daniel told her sympathetically as he took her camera from her and stowed it back in its bag.

"If that's the case then I think I'll give nature a miss for a while and spend more time in the office," she said as they picked their way out of the undergrowth. "Now that I've taken all the photos I need for the leaflets, I can work with Carl on those. Then I must concentrate on doing some cataloguing. I'm afraid I haven't managed to start that yet," she added apologetically.

"Not a problem. The leaflets have always been the priority. And the educational programme too. We need them both for the summer visitors."

She nodded moodily. She could still see the image of the tiny limp poult hanging from the hawk's sharp talons.

"Are you okay?" Daniel could see something was wrong.

"I'm fine," she said, and then she burst into tears.

"Hey, it's not that bad," Instantly his arms were around her. "It's just a wild turkey, not someone's dog. That hawk has a brood to feed, too, you know."

"I know it does! It just shocked me, the way it came out of nowhere. And now I feel such a fool," she sniffed, scrabbling around in her chinos for a tissue.

"Here, let me," he produced a wad of tissues from his pocket and, lifting her chin with one finger so that she was forced to look at him, wiped away her tears.

Coming to her senses she grabbed them from him. He was way too close! She couldn't cope with this as well. Her plan didn't work quite as she intended though, because he kept his arms around her as she scrubbed at her face, and didn't remove them until she gave him a watery smile.

"Better?" he asked, taking a step away from her.

She nodded. "Better, but very embarrassed."

"Well don't be. You've had to take in a lot since you arrived in Florida, and there's a way to go yet. You'll probably see worse than a dead poult before it's over."

Chapter Seventeen

After their trip to the State Reserve, Claire didn't see much of Daniel for several weeks. According to Beth another crisis had surfaced in the family business, and in the short periods when he was at home he spent most of his time meeting up with project teams from other conservancy organizations in order to swop ideas, and to try to identify new funding.

Part of her was glad he was away so much. It not only meant she could continue to visit his parents without worrying about him suddenly showing up, it also meant she could concentrate on her work without that permanent flutter in her stomach whenever he was around. The contrary side of her missed him however, so she often found herself glancing out of the window halfway through reading a document, hoping he would walk by and come in through the door behind her with a cheery greeting. It wasn't any better in her apartment either. When she wasn't busy meeting up with Scott, or Beth, or with one or two of the volunteers who had become her friends, she spent far too much time on her balcony watching the boats sailing by as she searched in vain for the one that had Daniel at the helm.

When he did finally turn up it was in a totally unexpected way. It was at the end of a long and busy week and she had just returned home from work and taken a shower when the doorbell rang. Wrapping a towel around her she went to answer it. A girl with long blonde hair was standing outside looking distinctly nervous.

"You must be Claire," she said. Then, without waiting for an answer, she rushed on. "I'm Taylor-Ann, Daniel's sister...you know, one of the ones still at college."

"I know who you are," Claire smiled at her. "Come on in while I put something on. Then I'll make some coffee."

"Oh no! I don't want to hold you up or anything. Really! I just want to invite you to a lunchtime barbecue tomorrow. Melanie and I are home for the summer break now and...well we've persuaded our parents to let us invite all our friends around so that we can catch up with the news...and my mother thought you might like to come too. She talks about you quite a lot," she added.

"That's so kind of you, but please come in just for a moment," Claire pleaded, liking her instantly whilst also wishing she didn't look quite so much like Daniel.

"Well...okay. But I told Dan I wouldn't be long. He's downstairs talking business with the manager of the apartment block. He said I could come too as long as I was quick."

Hiding the twist of pain she felt when she learned that Daniel was downstairs, but that he wouldn't be coming up to see her, Claire nodded. Then she held the door wide for Taylor-Ann and followed her inside.

With a cry of delight the younger girl made straight for the balcony and stood looking over the railing at the blue waters of the bay. "What a great view. You must love it here. I always forget how much I miss the sea until I'm back home again."

"I do...love it I mean," Claire called out from the bathroom, her voice muffled as she pulled a clean T-shirt over her head. Then, fastening her shorts, she padded barefoot back into the sitting room and out onto the balcony.

"Oh look, dolphins!" Taylor-Ann cried, gripping Claire's wrist in her excitement. "Wow! Daniel must think a lot of you to let you stay here and hog this view. This is his best development in Dolphin Key. I'm surprised he had an apartment free for the whole summer."

Claire stared at her but the other girl was too intent on the dolphins to be aware of the shock wave she had caused with her innocent remark. Not at all sure how to respond Claire finally opted for a safer subject.

"Daniel told me I would get used to the dolphins," she said. "But I haven't yet!"

Taylor-Ann turned to her with a grin. "Nor have I, and I was born here! Let's persuade him to take us out in his boat so we can follow them. It's tied up at the pier. Come on!"

She was halfway out of the door as she spoke and within moments Claire heard her voice echoing up through the stairwell as she ran down the stairs, calling out to Daniel as she went.

Unsure whether she should follow or not, Claire delayed making a decision by the simple dint of taking the time to brush her hair and put on some lip-gloss. By the time she had finished Taylor-Ann was calling up to her from beneath the balcony.

"Come on Claire! Daniel's waiting."

Leaning over the railing she looked down and found herself staring straight into Daniel's eyes. For a moment his expression didn't change, then he gave her a slow smile. "I see that my little sister has taken you in hand too!"

She smiled back, her heart thumping against her chest in an unseemly fashion. "Apparently so."

"You're coming then?"

"Of course. You know me and dolphins!" She thrust her feet into her thongs as she spoke and then, with a brief wave, disappeared from view.

By the time she reappeared on the beach, Daniel had managed to control the surge of feeling that had threatened to overwhelm him when she first peered over the edge of the balcony. He had deliberately kept his distance over the past weeks, only meeting with her when absolutely necessary and leaving everything else to Scott and Beth. He was glad for once to have the excuse of the family business to keep him away because, after the day they had spent together at the State Reserve, he no longer trusted himself.

Crouching next to her watching the wild turkeys had taught him that. Even as he talked about them and showed her where to look, he had been unable to tear his gaze away from her profile, or to ignore the fact that her body was pressed close to his as they attempted to remain out of sight behind the fallen tree. And then the hawk had swooped and she had surprised them both by bursting into tears.

Even now he cringed at his over-the-top response but he hadn't been able to help himself. His instinct had been to hold her close and he could still recall the warmth of her skin against his arm and the dewy softness of her cheeks as he wiped away her tears.

It had taken him a long time to get to sleep that night, and by the time the first fingers of dawn started to creep over the horizon he had decided he wasn't going to risk being alone with her again until he could find the time to date her properly. If she had responded in any way when he held her in his arms, then things might have been different, but she hadn't. And with Scott in the picture it wasn't likely to happen any time soon either. So he had bitten the bullet and just got on with his life, immersing himself in work in much the same way he'd done before she arrived. He hadn't asked about her either, even though Scott had kept him up to date with the work she was doing.

The only person he'd discussed her with was Carl, and that was when he saw the finished leaflets. The pictures were stunning and they both agreed she'd been right to persuade Scott to pose for them.

"Beth tells me that female visitor numbers are up already," Carl said with a grin as he handed Daniel a stack of leaflets to put in his car. "I don't believe her of course, she just said it to wind me up, to rub in the fact that Scott beats me on all counts…looks, brawn, and brains. And on top of that he's Mr Nice Guy too!"

Daniel laughed. "As if that would make any difference to Beth. *And* you know it!"

"I guess. It's a shame that Claire can't photograph herself as well though! A picture of the pair of them together would really bring in the punters, even people with no interest in wildlife whatsoever."

Daniel hid his misery as he smiled in agreement, because he knew that everything Carl said was true. Then, unable to help himself, he asked the question that had been hovering on the tip of his tongue from the moment he first entered the print shop. "Is there anything going on between them? Scott and Claire I mean."

"Don't ask me, ask Beth. She's the expert on such matters. The only thing I've noticed is that whenever one of them comes over for a meal, the other one comes too. I haven't seen much sign of romance though. It's more a case of good friends I think, but I could be wrong."

Daniel couldn't bring himself to ask Beth, however. Instead, he just kept away from the office as much as possible, unwilling to see anything that might blow away his gossamer thin hope that he still had some sort of a chance with Claire once he found the time to work on it. He even tried to persuade himself that he was keeping out of her way for a reason. That if he left her and Scott to themselves for a while, then they would tire of one another and Scott, as so often before, would start looking for a new conquest.

And now here she was standing in front of him, totally delectable in a striped T-shirt and white shorts, her long legs tanned to a pale biscuit colour by the sun. Next to her his pretty little sister looked just what she was, a college kid who was still experimenting with her identity; while Claire was all woman, someone who knew exactly who she was and who didn't need clothes and make-up to define her. He dragged his eyes away from her slender curves and pointed towards the pier.

"If you two climb on board I'll be with you in a couple of minutes. I just have to sign a few more things for the manager."

* * *

The trip was very different from the first one he and Claire had taken together. With Taylor-Ann on board it was impossible to make a peaceful loop around the bay searching for dolphins because every time she thought she saw one she shrieked her excitement.

"Look! Dan, look! There's one over there…can you see it? It's in a direct line out from the pier. Here, give me you binoculars."

Snatching them from his neck she held them up to her eyes, breathless with anticipation, only to lower them again with a dejected pout when she realized she had been looking at a pelican diving for its dinner, or a seagull bobbing on the water.

In the end Daniel lost patience with her. "For goodness sake, be quiet Taylor-Ann! Any dolphin we might have seen will have hightailed it out to sea by now, frightened away by the sound of your non-stop chattering."

"Chastened by his sharp tone, she looked about twelve years old as she handed back his binoculars with a sigh. "I'm sorry! It's just I get so excited when I first come home. You know I do. So does Melanie."

He reached over and gently pulled a long strand of her hair. "I know. But being excited and seeing dolphins don't go together. Now just be quiet, there's a good girl, and I'll see if I can find some for you."

Picking up an old baseball cap that was rolling around at the bottom of the dinghy, Taylor rammed it on her head, tucked her long hair up inside it, and did as she was told.

Claire watched, fascinated. Daniel might be Taylor-Ann's brother but he acted more like her father. True there was a really big age difference between them but it was something more than that. It was as if she expected him to take charge and tell her what to do. She guessed it was because his mother and father had more or less stopped functioning as proper parents years ago, leaving Daniel to shoulder almost every responsibility. She wondered how it made him feel. She was still pondering it when he slowed the dinghy almost to a standstill and pointed silently ahead.

At first Claire didn't see a thing but then the water sprayed into a million sparkling droplets as a pod of about eight dolphins leapt out of the water together, their skin like pewter in the late afternoon sunshine. Taylor, still silent, sat hunched at the front of the dinghy, her T-shirt pulled down over her bare legs, her eyes shining with excitement.

Claire's eyes met Daniel's and they smiled at one another. Then they looked back to where the dolphins were heading at speed across the bay. Nobody spoke until the final fin had disappeared from view in a splash of rainbow coloured spray. Only then, and without turning around from her lookout point at the stern, did Taylor-Ann break the silence.

"That was magical," she sighed. "Thank you Dan. Now I truly feel I'm home again."

"My pleasure," he said, pointing the dinghy back towards the pier and, as he did so, realizing that he suddenly felt very happy. Pleased as he was to have his sister at home again, he was under no illusion that his happiness had anything to do with her. No! It was because of the smile he had exchanged with Claire, out there amongst the dolphins. It had been a smile of mutual understanding, as if she somehow knew what his life was like, knew about all the responsibilities he had, all the balls he had to juggle, and understood and sympathized. And, unless he was deluding himself, there had been something else too. He was sure her gray eyes had held an invitation, and it was something he was going to follow up, Scott or not Scott, as soon as he had done his duty by his family.

* * *

When they arrived back at the pier they were greeted by Taylor-Ann's double. "That's Melanie," she told Claire, with an airy wave of her hand towards the girl leaning against the railings that surrounded the pier.

"I think I would have guessed that," Claire told her, laughing as she climbed out of the dinghy to say hello.

"Don't be fooled," Daniel called up from below, trying to concentrate on securing the dinghy instead of looking at Claire's legs disappearing up the ladder above him. "They might look alike, but Melanie is the sensible one. She doesn't talk as much as Taylor-Ann either."

"That is so not true!" Taylor-Ann pulled a face at him as he joined them on the pier. Melanie, however, merely smiled.

He kissed her cheek. "Where have you been? It's not like you to disappear when you first arrive home. I was expecting the pair of you to pester me until I agreed to take you out in the dinghy."

"Oh around and about...I had a few people to see," Melanie's voice was quieter than her sister's, her eyes more solemn. "I'm ready to go home now though. Do you think dinner will be ready? I'm starving!"

"Probably. Come on then." He clambered back down into the dinghy and held it steady while they joined him.

Claire watched them go with a smile. "Don't forget the barbecue tomorrow," Taylor-Ann called as Daniel started up the engine. "It starts at twelve."

"I'll be there," Claire waved goodbye, her eyes locking with Daniel's one last time before he turned away and headed out into the bay. Even as her heart flipped she wondered whether he had noticed that Melanie's answer had been elusive, and that she had changed the subject as to her whereabouts very quickly. Somehow she didn't think he had.

She walked away from the pier deep in thought. What was his sister up to, and did Taylor-Ann know? Had she deliberately kept Daniel occupied so that Melanie could visit someone she knew he wouldn't approve of, or was she just imagining the whole thing?

It wasn't long before she found out because when she got back to her apartment Scott was sitting on her doorstep waiting for her. She stared at him in surprise.

"What are you doing here? I thought you said you had a date tonight."

"I did…have one I mean…except she had to go home early to have dinner with her family."

Claire frowned as everything clicked into place. "It was Melanie wasn't it? She was your date. How come you never told me you were dating her?

Then, remembering Melanie's behavior when Daniel questioned her, she shook her head. "It's a secret isn't it? You and Melanie are meeting in secret."

He leapt to his feet in horror. "How did you know? I didn't think anyone knew about us. Melanie is so paranoid about her family finding out I've had to promise to keep it under wraps. It's not something I'm happy about either, especially as far as Daniel is concerned"

"I'm sure you're not…but don't worry, as far as I know your secret's safe. I just guessed Scott."

He groaned as he tugged at his hair with anxious fingers. "If you've guessed then it won't be long before someone else does too."

"Not necessarily. I just happened to meet up with her a few minutes ago, and there was something about the way she spoke to Daniel that made me think she didn't want him to know where she had been and what she had been doing. If you hadn't turned up on my doorstep immediately afterwards and told me your date had gone home early, then I would never have put two and two together."

"Well now you do know it makes it easier for me to ask a favor."

She unlocked her door and held it wide. "Come in and have a beer. You look as if you need one."

He followed her inside and threw himself down on the couch while she busied herself pouring out two beers and tipping some nuts and olives into a couple of bowls.

"Bring those out onto the balcony," she told him. "I want to watch the sunset even if you don't."

He did as she asked and then slumped low in one of the chairs she kept on the balcony and propped feet on the wooden balustrade. "It's all such a mess," he said dejectedly, tipping his glass and swallowing half his beer.

"I suppose you and Melanie are seeing one another in secret because she's worried her parents won't approve?"

"Yeah...something like that, and she's got a point. They'll say I'm too old for her, that I don't earn nearly enough money to support us, that she's still at college...that she's just a kid, except...except she's not."

Claire gave an inward sigh as she heard the pain in his voice. Was there no end to the bleak undercurrents that swirled around the Marchant family? "Daniel wouldn't react like that," she said.

"Don't kid yourself! He would be even worse. To him Taylor-Ann and Melanie *are* just kids. He won't accept they've grown up and, although it bugs me, I can sort of understand it. Ever since Mr Marchant lost his sight Daniel has had to run the family business. He makes all the financial decisions too. And he's the one who is putting the twins through college. He's the one who set Carl up in business as well. And he's also the one who does his best to stop his mother giving in to complete despair. So it's not surprising he has started thinking like a father instead of a brother. I'm sure he's just looking out for them when he tells them they are too young to be romantically involved with anyone…but it doesn't make it easy for me, or for Melanie."

"So what is the favour?" Claire's heart sank as she spoke because she was sure she wasn't going to like it, whatever it was.

"I want you to come to the barbecue with me tomorrow," Scott's eyes shifted away from her in embarrassment when she looked across at him. "I know it's a big ask, but if I arrive with you then it will allay everyone's suspicion and take the pressure of Melanie. Please say yes Claire, because I must see her."

Chapter Eighteen

Busy flipping burgers, as well as taking care the steaks didn't burn, Daniel had little chance to talk to Scott and Claire when they arrived at the barbecue. Not that he wanted to talk to them, not after last night.

He had just finished eating dinner with his parents and sisters when the manager of Claire's apartment block had called his cell phone. Apologising for disturbing him, the man explained he had forgotten to give him some papers for a forthcoming meeting. He offered to bring them over but Daniel told him he would collect them. Promising to arrive early the following morning to help set up the barbecue, he kissed his mother and sisters goodbye. Then, with a brief farewell to his father, he strode out across the deck and down to where he had tied up his dinghy.

As he set off across the bay he gave a sigh of relief. So far, so good! His father had been reasonably pleasant to Taylor-Ann and Melanie. There had been no second thoughts about the barbecue, no suggestion he was anything other than pleased to have them home again. And because he was being cooperative his mother had lost her hunted look and begun to relax and to enjoy the girls' stories about college and their friends. It was probably too much to expect that things would stay that way all summer but he could at least hope. In the meantime it was good to escape the confines of family and responsibility and think, instead, of Claire.

His heart lifted as he puttered across the bay. The memory of the smile she had given him earlier wouldn't go away. He was sure he had seen an invitation in her eyes. Maybe Carl was right and she and Scott were just friends. Maybe it was time he made a move. After all, she had been in Dolphin Key for long enough now for it to seem an entirely natural progression. Later, if there was a later, he would admit he had enticed her to Florida for entirely selfish reasons, but right now getting her to agree to a date was the first thing he had to do. He would ask her tomorrow, at the barbecue. No, he had a better idea. He would act right now, before he got cold feet. As soon as he had collected the papers that were waiting for him, he would go up to her apartment, knock on the door, and invite her out.

With a smile of relief now he had made his decision, he glanced up at her balcony. His heart plummeted like a stone when he saw Scott sitting there. Although he couldn't see Claire very clearly, it was obvious that they were sitting very close together. Then he had seen Scott wrap his arm around her shoulders and hug her. After that he had stopped watching. So much for the invitation he was sure he had seen in her eyes. It was nothing more than his imagination going into overdrive.

And now here they were again, at the barbecue. They had arrived together. They were sitting together, and they appeared to be very happy. With a sigh he turned back to his cooking. At least he had something to occupy him, something to take his mind off the heart-wrenching sight of them laughing together.

* * *

"Hello. You look as if you could do with some help." He heard the amusement in her voice, as he swung round to face her.

"Are you offering?" Smiling at her was an effort but he managed it.

"I am actually. And you had better take me up on it because I seem to be your only option."

He laughed, and it was a genuine laugh this time. The lawns and the deck were swarming with people, most of them young, all of them intent on enjoying themselves. Even his father was smiling at something that Taylor-Ann was saying, while his mother was busy setting out salads and baskets of bread on the long table set up in the lozenge of shade provided by the side of the house.

"I guess I'll say yes then."

For the next twenty minutes they worked side-by-side without talking as they served meat onto plates, and piled onions, relish, burgers and sausages into split rolls. Finally, the last person had been served and, with a sigh of relief, Claire wiped her hands on a paper napkin.

Daniel put a piece of sirloin steak and a sausage onto a plate and handed it to her. "Here…it's your turn now. Go and get yourself some salad. It's time you got back to your date."

"My date? Oh, you mean Scott. I don't think he's missed me at all."

He followed her gaze and saw Scott sitting with Taylor-Ann, Melanie and some of their friends. From his hand gestures it was obvious he was explaining something to them. They all appeared to be hanging onto his every word.

"It's a good job he's with you because the twins and their friends are at just the right age to be far too susceptible to his good looks and charm," he told her, trying to keep any hint of bitterness out of his voice as he turned back to the barbecue and began to pile his own plate with food.

"He's really not *that* bad!" Claire sounded defensive as they walked across the grass together. "And he can't help how he looks."

Nor can you thought Daniel as he glanced at her. She looked cool and fresh in a blue sundress that swirled about her ankles. Her toenails, which were peeping out from flat, strappy sandals, were painted a deep cerise color.

As they approached the table, she changed the subject. "Something that Taylor-Ann said yesterday has been bothering me Daniel. I need to know…I need you to tell me why you let Beth arrange for me to stay in one of your best holiday rentals instead of hiring it out for the summer?"

Startled by her unexpected question, he stopped in the act of reaching for some bread and looked at her. Her eyes blazed blue in the sunlight as she waited for his answer.

"Because I wanted you to enjoy living in Dolphin Key, I guess," he told her after a long pause while he searched for a plausible answer. After all he could hardly tell her it was because he always wanted her to have the best of everything he could ever offer her, not when her date was sitting just a short distance away on the grass.

She looked at him doubtfully. "Why did you think I wouldn't enjoy it if I lived somewhere else?"

"I didn't…that is, I was sure you would…but you have only signed a contract for six months remember, and I wanted to find a way to keep you here for longer than that. Surely you can see why. Now that you have settled into the job you must be able to see that there is still a lot for you to do."

"Well, yes, of course I can. But I can't go on living where I do, not now I know how much it's costing you."

"Yes you can! The apartment is part of the job package Claire. It's yours for as long as you stay here."

Startled by the vehemence in his voice, she opened her mouth to protest, but before she had a chance to speak Taylor-Ann interrupted them.

"Hey you two, are you going to stand here all day, or are you coming over to join us? Scott's been telling us about the photos you took of him Claire. He's pretending he's mad at you but we know he's not really."

Claire glanced across to where Scott was sitting. Melanie was next to him but they were angled slightly away from another, and each of them was talking to a different group of people. At a quick glance their proximity to one another appeared to be entirely innocent. There was no eye contact, their bodies weren't touching, and yet…there *was* something. She frowned slightly. Then she realized what it was. Half hidden in the long grass, their fingers were entwined. She took two swift paces and sat down beside them, making sure that the swirling folds of her dress covered their hands.

"You idiot!" she hissed into Scott's ear as she pretended to settle herself comfortably next to him.

He gave her a grateful smile. "Thanks. I didn't think."

Because he kept his voice low, and because his face was turned towards her, the two of them looked as if they were having an intimate conversation. It pierced Daniel's heart to see them sitting so close together, apparently oblivious to everyone else around them. Unable to bear the thought of watching them for the rest of the afternoon, he made an excuse and walked away.

Claire watched him go. He looked so lonely as he made his way across the lawn to where his parents were sitting in the shade. She wished she could join them but she couldn't break her promise to Scott. With a sigh she tuned into the conversation going on around her, knowing that she was deluding herself anyway. For a moment yesterday as they sailed across the bay in search of dolphins, she had thought things were about to change between them...but now, by walking away, he had made it perfectly clear that he wasn't even interested in spending the afternoon with her. So the sooner she gave up wishing for something that was never going to happen, the better.

* * *

People started to leave towards the end of the afternoon and by then Claire had had more than enough of acting as chaperone. "Come on. It's time we helped your mother to clear up," she said to Melanie, picking up her own plate and glass and getting to her feet.

Melanie did the same, but with reluctance.

Claire smiled sympathetically. "Scott will still be here when we've finished because he can't leave without me. I'm his date, remember!"

"I know and I'm sorry you're involved," the younger girl's eyes brimmed with sudden tears that she dashed away with the back of her hand. Then she looked at Claire. "What would you do in my place?"

"I would talk to my parents…and to Daniel. And I'd get Scott to talk to them too. They're far more likely to agree that you can date one another if you're honest with them, whereas if they catch you sneaking out to see him they might be very angry with both of you. You're not even being fair to Scott, Melanie, because you know he doesn't want to keep it a secret."

"But what if it doesn't work like that. What if they throw me out? What if Daniel sacks Scott?" Melanie looked agonized.

Claire stared at her. "Whatever makes you think any of that would happen?"

"Carl! They did it with Carl didn't they? He had to leave home, and now Dad won't see him, won't even allow his name to be mentioned. He's won't let him work in the family business either, even though everyone knows that he would be really good at it."

Aware that this was a conversation they needed to have alone, Claire grabbed a handful of trash bags. Thrusting some into Melanie's hands she led her away from where groups of people were still chatting, to an area on the far side of the garden. Once there she began to collect discarded paper plates and napkins, and scraps of uneaten food.

"The problems with Carl were entirely different Melanie," she said quietly. "He chose to do something that disrupted the plans your father had for him, whereas you only want to date someone when you are home from college."

Melanie bent down and began to pick up some crusts of bread that were scattered across the grass, but she wasn't swift enough to hide the blush that rose to the roots of her hair.

Claire looked down at her. Her heart sank as she suddenly realized Melanie's relationship with Scott was far more serious than a summer romance. This was way beyond her pay grade. What Daniel's family, and Scott, for that matter, chose to do with their private lives was not her business…she needed to walk away from this…she was searching around for the words that would extract her from what was fast becoming a difficult situation when she suddenly remembered what Scott had told her the previous evening. He had said that Daniel had been looking after his whole family for years; that it was entirely thanks to him the twins were getting a college education and that all the family's medical bills were being paid. It was down to him as well that his parents were still enjoying a comfortable lifestyle. And then, of course, there was Carl. Daniel had set Carl up in business, even though he had neglected to tell her so when he gave her the potted version of his family's history, the night they sat on his deck in the moonlight.

She remembered, too, how kind he had always been to her, how special her apartment was. Finally she acknowledged how, against her better judgment, he had persuaded her to take a job that was exactly the right one for her, and in that moment she knew she owed him. She knew she had to do whatever was needed to help him, even if it was something she didn't consider her business. Daniel might not be interested in having a relationship with her, but he was her friend as well as her employer, and she never turned her back on her friends. With an inward sigh she confronted Melanie.

"Scott visits you at college, doesn't he?" she asked.

Melanie nodded wordlessly. Then she looked up at Claire with an abject expression on her face. "Please don't tell Daniel…or my parents. I know you visit them…I know you're friends with Dan…but please don't tell them Claire."

"I have no intention of telling anyone anything, but I do think you and Scott need to have a serious talk about your relationship. You can't keep it a secret forever you know, and it will be much, much worse for Scott if Daniel finds out he's been deceiving him."

"I know how much he hates not telling him," Melanie admitted. "It's just I'm frightened that telling will spoil everything, and make things worse at home too. Mum can barely cope as it is. She just lives for when Taylor-Ann and I come home, and we try really hard to keep things sweet for her when we're here by not upsetting Dad."

"I understand all of that," Claire assured her. "But I still think you've got to take the chance. Surely you can see how much worse the alternative is. How, by risking being found out, you are jeopardizing everything; your relationships with Scott, with your parents, even with Daniel, because he would never trust you, or Scott, ever again.

"I know you're right, and I *will* do it, I promise." Tears trickled down Melanie's cheeks as she straightened up, but the look she gave Claire was a determined one, even though her eyes were clouded with fear. Then she saw Scott approaching and she gave a watery smile as he walked across the lawn towards them.

"Here comes the muscle, just in time to collapse the trestle table."

Claire laughed in spite of herself and picked up a solitary tray that had been abandoned on the grass. "I guess I can trust the two of you to clear up the rest of this part of the garden together while I collect up some glasses and take them indoors."

Scott shot her a grateful look.

"But ask Melanie what we've been talking about while you do it," she called over her shoulder as she walked away.

* * *

Daniel was pacing up and down and talking on his cell phone when Claire finally returned to the garden. She had spent some time stacking

217

the dishwasher and helping to pack away the uneaten food. Now all she wanted to do was to leave without having to talk to Daniel. Seeing he was deep in conversation she gave a sigh of relief as she raised a hand in farewell and started to search for Scott. Instead of acknowledging that she was going, however, Daniel beckoned her towards him. She sighed. Now what?

She had already said goodbye to Taylor-Ann, and to Mrs Marchant, and she had promised Mr Marchant she would visit again the following week to read to him. They were now on their fourth book, a thriller this time, and one that was considerably more interesting than the previous three. She was fast becoming frustrated with him, however, because his resistance to the Talking Books service was as strong as ever, despite his earlier promise to consider it.

"What would you do if I stopped reading to you?" she had asked him the last time she visited.

"I would ask my wife to resume her duties," he replied, with no sense whatsoever of how his domineering attitude was making his wife's life a misery.

Claire had given up and resumed reading, but without the sense of enjoyment that reading aloud usually gave her. He was so arrogant and overbearing that she frequently wondered why she bothered at all. But when she saw how much he enjoyed it, and how much it helped Mrs Marchant, she always promised to return.

"Claire, I need a favour," Daniel said, cutting his call and returning his cell to his pocket as he walked towards her.

Not you too! The thought brought a fleeting feeling of resentment until she saw the worry in his eyes.

"I've just found out that Carl and I have to go away for a couple of days next week to sort out a problem ...but Beth...the baby"

"Is due in a couple of weeks, I know."

Yes. And...well you know how it is with my parents. The twins wouldn't be much help either...so do you think... that is, would you mind just keeping an eye on her while we're away?"

"If she'll let me." Claire frowned as she thought of Beth. Although her pregnancy was now obvious, her bump was still small and neat and she didn't seem to have made any adjustments to her life. She still walked at top speed, she still worked the same hours for Daniel, she still helped Carl in the print shop, and when she wasn't doing any of that, she still spent all her spare time painting.

She had already given Claire a watercolor, a view of the wooden remnants of the old pier with brown pelicans roosting on every spar. It was beautifully executed and there was humor in it too. Claire had been delighted but she had also protested when Beth gave it to her, saying she should sell it in the local gallery where it would be snapped up by one of the many visitors who mooched amongst the artifacts and paintings looking for a memento of their holiday. But Beth had been adamant.

"I painted it for you because I know how much you love watching the pelicans," she said. "Besides, I don't want to paint for the gallery. I want to open my own studio and sell stuff straight from there…you know, the 'come and see a working artist and buy her pictures' sort if thing. And I'll do it too, just as soon as we've made a go of the print shop."

"I thought you already had," Claire was surprised.

Beth pulled a face. "It brings in enough for us to live on, but there's nothing left over. No matter! We're getting there."

And that had been the end of the conversation. Claire had thanked her and taken the painting home, hung it on the wall, and derived a great deal of pleasure from looking at it without giving any more thought to Beth's situation.

Now, however, seeing the concern on Daniel's face, she felt a twinge of dismay. Why did Carl have to go away with Daniel? Was he in trouble again or was it just a business trip? Was his and Beth's print business okay?"

Unable to ask Daniel any of the numerous questions that popped into her head, she started to think about something else that was equally confusing. Was he worried about Beth being on her own for Carl's sake, or was it because he still loved her himself? She guessed she would never know.

"I'll do my best," she conceded. "Although I can't promise I'll be successful because she's the most independent person I know."

He gave a relieved smile. "Thank you. I'll tell Carl. If we could avoid leaving her, believe me we would. And if there are any problems at all, then please just call me, any time, day or night…because one thing is for sure, Beth won't! She'll try to cope on her own."

Something inside Claire wouldn't let her return his smile. She didn't know whether she was jealous because he was so worried about Beth, or whether it was pique because he hadn't chosen to join her during the afternoon. Whatever it was, her lips refused to curve upwards. Instead, she just nodded, and then turned away so that he wouldn't see the frustration in her eyes.

In a month or so she was going to have to decide whether she was going to stay in Dolphin Bay, or whether she was going to return to England at the end of her six-month contract, because although she loved her job, and thoroughly enjoyed her new life, she wasn't sure she could continue working with Daniel. She had tried to accept that he wasn't interested in her. She had made other friends and developed a social life, but none of it had made a jot of difference. Her mouth still grew dry whenever she saw him and her pulse became erratic as soon as she heard his voice. It seemed as if her first thought about moving to Florida to work with him had been the right one after all. Her heart sank. Whether she liked it or not, soon it would be time to go home.

* * *

Daniel watched her walk away with a frown. Had he been presumptuous in asking her to keep an eye on Beth? He knew they were good friends, so he had been sure Claire would want to know Beth was on her own so near to the end of her pregnancy. Not that he and Carl intended to be away for a moment longer than necessary, but this trip was something they had to make together.

He sighed as he started to clean up the barbecue. If only it didn't have to be this way but, despite many warnings, his father had brought it on himself. It was no longer possible to run the company the way he wanted it. Times had moved on. Finances were difficult. Clients wanted different experiences. Yet whenever Daniel or the other directors suggested changes, Gordon Marchant always managed to thwart them, and because he was still Chairman of the company there was little they could do about it unless they ousted him from the Board.

For months it had been clear that unless drastic action was taken, and soon, the company would fold, and they would all go down with it. Not wanting to destroy what was left of his father's pride, Daniel had managed to avoid making a final decision until the fire in Mexico.

That had been the final straw, however, and, even worse, so had his father's reaction. Instead of recognising that in the wake of such a disaster the company needed to rebuild its reputation with further investment and with special promotional deals, he had spent all his time trying to apportion blame. This had resulted in the very public resignation of one of the company's best resort managers. A particularly unpleasant meeting with him had left Daniel feeling emotionally bruised and beyond weary, and ready, finally, to accept that the time had come to do the one thing he had been trying to avoid. He had nowhere else to go. His only solution was to call for a special Board Meeting and ask for a vote of no confidence in his own father, the person who had originally set up the company. To do this he had to present the directors with a solution to their present dilemma and this was where Carl came in. It was the reason why they needed to attend the Board Meeting together.

He stopped scraping the barbecue and stared into space as he thought about his brother. Carl had proved to be a source of unexpected wisdom and support over the past couple of years. Back on track thanks to Beth, he had found the strength to leave his past behind and make a new life. In the process he had discovered that he not only had a good business brain, and a flair for negotiation, but he was a natural salesman too. And if Beth was added to the mix, with her eye for color and décor, and her enormous energy, then the new leaders of Marchant Enterprises were standing in the wings ready to take over. All Daniel had to do was persuade the Board that this was the way forward.

He looked over to where his father was sitting alone on the deck waiting for his wife to come to his aid, and his heart shriveled inside him. He didn't want to do this to him and yet he knew he had to, for everyone's sake. If he didn't, then his parents would have to sell the house they had lived in and cherished for so long, and move to somewhere much smaller. Taylor-Ann and Melanie would have to finish college too, and find some sort of employment, and he would have to think long and hard about whether he could afford to keep his own company going or whether he should abandon it and look for another job. One that would bring in the sort of rewards the family needed to survive. He tried not to think about what would happen if he abandoned his own dreams because he knew it would break his heart. He also knew it would mean saying goodbye to Claire as well.

He looked around the garden wondering if she was still around or whether she had already left. He wished he could take her into his confidence, but there was no way he could possibly burden her with such a secret, especially as she visited his parents so frequently. Eventually he spotted her. She was standing on the far side of the lawn talking to Melanie. Scott was standing beside her and the three of them seemed to be having a serious discussion about something. Then, as he watched, Claire and Scott turned away with a brief smile and a wave. Within moments they had gone, leaving him feeling more miserable than he had ever felt in his life.

Chapter Nineteen

Over the next few days Claire felt increasingly despondent. Gone was any hope Daniel might suddenly see her in a new light and decide he really did want to have a date with her after all. Gone, too, was the carefree friendship she had had with Scott. He was far too busy spending time with Melanie, and worrying about what would happen when she told her parents about her relationship with him, to give any thought to Claire. Nor was Beth her usual cheerful self. She seemed to have something on her mind but whatever it was, she didn't share it. Instead she just kept her head down when she was in the office, and left with little more than a brief farewell on the dot of five o'clock.

To add to her misery, the weather was so hot and humid she found it difficult to concentrate. Even the air conditioning in her apartment was a mixed blessing because it kept her awake at night with its constant humming and yet if she turned it off the growing heat was unbearable, so when Daniel called her on his first day away, to check if Beth was okay, her reply was brusque to the point of rudeness, something she regretted the moment she cut the connection.

Angry with herself, as well as with everyone else, her state of mind began to affect how she felt about her job as well, and she took to leaving on time like Beth, instead of staying to chat about work with Scott. Consequently she had been home for several hours on the day Beth telephoned her.

"Claire...would you like to come over for a couple of hours?"

When Claire heard the uncharacteristic quaver in her friend's voice she was instantly alert. "What's wrong?"

"Nothing...it's just that Carl's away...and I think there's a hurricane brewing."

By now Claire had been well briefed about hurricanes, and about their history in the Dolphin Bay area. She knew it was very unlikely they would have a direct hit but she also knew it *was* possible, so Beth's words made her feel doubly nervous.

"Would you like me to stay over?" she asked, fighting to make the question sound casual and to keep her voice calm.

"Um...yes, I...that would be great! Better to be together than both on our own if the weather does blow up."

It was obvious Beth was trying to hide her relief, but she didn't fool Claire. Something was wrong, so the sooner she set off for the apartment over the print shop, the better.

"Give me twenty minutes and I'll be with you," she said.

In less than ten minutes she had thrown overnight necessities and a change of clothes into a backpack, checked the contents of her fridge, and added a handful of herbal teabags to her luggage. Her packing complete, she brought the furniture in from the balcony, and locked and shuttered all the doors and windows. Then, with a final look around, she picked up the backpack, slung her camera case across her shoulder, stuffed her cell phone into her pocket, and made her way downstairs into the street.

The strength of the wind startled her, as did the size of the waves curling up through the bay. She had never seen the sea behave like that before. Ever since she'd arrived in Dolphin Bay the water had been so calm the fisherman considered even a mild swell to be a bad day. Pushing down a rising panic she battled her way across to Main Street and then turned left and hurried towards the print shop as fast as she could.

Beth was waiting for her. She opened the door as soon as Claire tugged on the rope of the ship's bell that hung over the doorway, and pulled her inside.

"According to the guys at the National Hurricane Centre it's going to give us a wide berth. We'll just have high winds for a couple of days, and some rain. It might disrupt travel though…" her voice trailed off as she stared dejectedly at Claire.

"So you're worried about Carl and Daniel," Claire finished the sentence for her.

"I'm not worried about *them*. I know they won't travel if there's any danger...it's more that I'm worried they won't be able to get home in time."

"In time for what?" Claire looked puzzled until the penny dropped, and then she started to worry. "You mean the baby. Are you in labour Beth?"

"I...I don't know...that is, I'm not sure. I've still got two weeks to go and because I've never had a baby before I don't really know what to expect. It might just be normal, this slight discomfort."

Exhibiting a calm exterior when she was actually cold with panic inside was something that came naturally to Claire. It was a skill she had developed as a child whenever she was faced with something new and scary, and now it kicked in automatically. She smiled encouragingly at Beth as she directed her back up the stairs to her homely and comfortable sitting room and settled her into a chair before she went into the kitchen to make herbal tea for both of them. While she was waiting for the kettle to boil she checked all the windows, securing the shutters, lowering the blinds and pulling the curtains until she had turned the apartment into a cozy cocoon.

"Drink this," she told Beth, handing her a mug of chamomile tea. "My mother swears by it. She says there's nothing better for soothing nerves and keeping panic at bay."

"Well let's hope your mother is right because panic is quite close," Beth gave her a watery smile as she raised the mug to her lips. "My mother died when I was small so I don't have any maternal wisdom to fall back on. I never really bonded with my stepmother either. It's my own fault. I never gave her a chance. I left home when she moved in although not for any particular reason. It just seemed the right thing to do at the time. And now my father is dead too, so…well it's just me…and Carl…and I really, really wish he was here."

"I'm so sorry. I didn't realize," Claire sank down onto one of the large cushions that furnished most of the room and put her mug on the floor.

"Usually it's OK," Beth told her with a sigh. "After all it happened a very long time ago and my life has moved on. In fact I rarely think about my mother at all, or I didn't until I found out I was pregnant. Since then...well, it's as if there's a hole in my life that can't be filled. If there was a time when she needed to stay around for me, then it's right now…instead of which I've got to do this on my own. She'll never see my baby either, nor will its other grandparents, given how Carl's parents feel about him…us."

Claire's heart went out to her. How could Mr and Mrs Marchant do this to her, to Carl, to their own flesh and blood? Did they even know about Beth's fractured family and, if they did, then where was their compassion? She didn't let her thoughts show, however. Instead she took another leaf out of her mother's book and became practical.

"Do you have everything ready in case you need to go to the hospital?"

Mutely, Beth shook her head.

"In that case, tell me what I need to pack and where it is. We may as well be prepared just in case."

* * *

Much later, having insisted that a weary looking Beth should go to bed, Claire lay dozing on the couch, listening to the wind. She had changed into her pajamas but it was too hot for covers. She wished she could open the windows but she knew it was impossible. She wished Carl and Daniel were here too. Having seen how scared Beth was, she didn't care any longer if Daniel was still in love with her. If Carl could accept it and remain his brother's best friend, then she was going to accept it as well.

It was her last thought as she drifted into a restless sleep. She was woken in the early hours of the morning by the sound of movement in the bathroom.

She returned to full consciousness with a start and knocked on the bathroom door. "Are you okay Beth?"

The door opened and Beth's frightened face looked up at her. "The baby *is* coming Claire. I know that now."

Claire took one look at her and saw the difference. A few hours ago she had just looked worried and confused, whereas now, despite being scared, she had an inward focus. Reaching for her cell phone Claire scrolled down to the number she had keyed in earlier, the one she had found at the top of Beth's maternity notes. When her call was answered she explained the situation, listened to a whole list of instructions, and then ended the call with a brief murmur of thanks.

Beth, meantime, had slipped down from the couch and was curled across one of the large cushions that furnished the room, breathing hard. After a minute or so she surprised Claire by looking up at her with an unexpected grin.

"If this is it, then I think I'll pass," she said.

Claire smiled at her. "Too late for that now, and you've got to be brave too because the person I spoke to at the maternity center says we need to stay here. She says it's too wild outside for us to tackle a fifty-minute journey with you in labor. But don't worry," she added swiftly, seeing the growing panic on Beth's face. "A couple of midwives are on their way and they have told me what to do until they get here."

* * *

For what seemed an eternity Claire used every skill she had to keep Beth calm and focused, gladder than she had ever thought she would be about the year her parents had decided to decamp to Southern Ireland to live the rural idyll. They had ended up renting a cottage next door to a pregnant woman who already had seven children under ten years old. When she went into labour her husband was working a hundred miles away, so it was Claire's mother who took charge, acting as temporary midwife while Claire's father went for medical help, and while Claire looked after the rest of the children.

Although she hadn't actually been present at the birth, the experience had taught Claire a great deal about children, about babies and, more especially, about women in labour. She remembered how her mother had rubbed the woman's back. She remembered, too, her mother encouraging the woman to pant through her contractions. Hiding her own growing panic as the minutes ticked by and no help arrived, she encouraged Beth to do the same, breathing and panting with her to help her through each contraction.

And in the gaps between she did what her mother had done, she rubbed Beth's back. She talked to her, too, promising everything would be all right, and telling her that help would soon arrive; although by the time Beth's contractions were barely a minute apart she was beginning to have her doubts. Pushing such thoughts to the back of her mind she began to prepare for the worst. In the brief moments when Beth didn't need her, she boiled water, collected towels, spread a clean sheet on the bed and added more pillows to the pile already there. Then she resumed her position beside the cushion in the sitting room where Beth said she felt most comfortable.

The thunderous knock on the door startled both of them, but only for a moment, and then Claire was taking the stairs two at a time, anxious to hand over her responsibilities to people who knew what they were doing. A tall man and a much smaller woman were standing outside, their arms full of medical paraphernalia.

"Are we in time?" They were already past her and half way up the stairs as they asked the question.

"Yes…but only just I think," she told them, slamming the door against a sudden gust of wind that threatened to take it off its hinges.

* * *

Beth's baby was born an hour later, and as the midwife placed him, still naked and slippery, onto his mother's stomach, Claire's tears spilled over. She had stayed with Beth throughout the labor. She had held her hand and encouraged her to push. She had brushed back the damp tangle of her hair and kept her forehead cool with a wet flannel. And now it was all over and the baby was perfect. He was dark, like Carl, and the ferocious frown of the newborn screwed up his face.

"He's just beautiful," she told Beth, wiping her eyes. Then she took a few photos with her cell phone before unpacking her camera in order to take some high quality pictures.

Beth smiled at her with a new radiance as she held out her arms for her new son. The midwife wrapped him in a clean towel and handed him to her. Then she and her assistant busied themselves tidying up while Claire took picture after picture of mother and baby as they gazed wonderingly at one another. It wasn't until she had finished that Beth asked about Carl and Daniel.

Claire shook her head. "I'm sorry Beth. I've been calling Daniel for hours but his cell isn't picking up. I've left a whole string of voice mail messages though, so we should hear from them as soon as they have a signal."

Beth's eyes filled with tears. "It wasn't meant to be like this. Carl was meant to be here with me."

"I know he was. It was just bad luck that you went into labor early."

"It wasn't bad luck. It was all my own fault." Beth shook her head as she shifted the baby into a more comfortable position. "He arrived early because I let that old goat who calls himself Carl's father upset me!"

"I don't think it happens like that. Babies come when they're ready, not because their mothers are upset," Claire did her best to reassure her, but Beth wouldn't listen. Instead the worry and fear she had been keeping shut up inside her burst out, and she began to talk.

Claire listened in growing horror as she learned about the trouble the family business was in, and how the only way it had a chance of being saved was for Daniel and Carl to get their father removed from the Board.

"The last few weeks have been dreadful," Beth told her. "So much so, that in the end I decided I would go and see Carl's parents. I thought if I made the first move I might be able to put things right, persuade my father-in-law to let go of the reins maybe."

She saw the expression on Claire's face and sighed. "I know! I know! I accept it was a stupid idea, but I had to try because Carl and Daniel are worried that removing him from the Board will destroy their father…and it's tearing them apart!"

She paused for a moment and looked down at her own new son. When she spoke again her voice held a mix of puzzlement and despair. "I just don't understand how he can behave like he does. How can anyone do what he is doing to both of his sons and not care about it?

"Does Carl know that you went to see him?"

"No. Nor does Daniel, and you mustn't tell them. They must never know the things he said about Carl; about how he wasn't fit to father a child; about how any child of ours was likely to end up on drugs and worse. Of course my mother-in-law wasn't around. If she had been he wouldn't have said such terrible things, but she was having a coffee with Carl at the print shop. You see I deliberately chose my time. I thought if I visited him alone I might be able to appeal to his better nature. Stupid of me to think that he had one," she added bitterly.

Claire was relieved when the midwife and her assistant came back into the room and said they needed to check Beth and the baby. She wanted Beth to enjoy her first hours with her little boy, not obsess about her father-in-law's cruelty. He had already done enough damage.

"I'll go and get us all something to eat," she said.

Glad to have something practical to do to counteract her growing anger, Claire rummaged through Beth's cupboards until she found enough ingredients to put together several rounds of sandwiches. She added cakes and biscuits, and some fruit, piled the whole lot onto a tray and carried it through to the sitting room. Then, because the others were still busy, she scrolled down to the cell phone pictures she had taken of Beth and the baby and sent them across the ether to Daniel, hoping against hope he would pick up soon.

* * *

By the time he finally called, Beth was asleep and Claire was sitting on the sofa cradling the baby. He had stirred just as Beth's eyes began to close, and the midwife had handed him to Claire and told her to try to keep him quiet for an hour or so while Beth got some rest. Then, barely pausing long enough to check Claire knew enough about small babies, and new mothers, to be left in charge of both of them, she and her colleague had rushed off to another emergency.

"Claire! It's Daniel." The connection was so poor she missed one word in three. He did manage to make her understand that he and Carl were on their way home, however, and that they hoped to be back in Dolphin Key by lunchtime.

With a sigh of relief she put down her cell phone and looked at the sleeping baby. "Your Daddy will be here to see you soon," she told him, gently stroking his cheek. "And your Uncle Daniel will want to see you too," she added, feeling as if her heart were about to break as she said the words out loud.

She didn't want to be around to see the pain Daniel would feel when he met his new nephew for the first time. To all outward appearances he might have got over his relationship with Beth, but the concern she had heard in his voice when he spoke to her on the phone told her otherwise, and she was quite sure the sight of Carl and Beth's new baby would bring it all back.

* * *

"Was that Carl?" Beth called from the bedroom.

238

"It was Daniel. He said they'll be here by lunchtime," Claire told her, carrying the baby back into the bedroom. "And as soon as they arrive I'm going to leave you all and go and tell Mr and Mrs Marchant and the twins the good news."

Beth stared up at her. There was something in Claire's face that spelled trouble but, before she could question her, the baby started to cry, and soon Beth was too wrapped up in motherhood to remember anything about it at all.

Chapter Twenty

True to their promise, Daniel and Carl
turned up at midday. By then, taking advantage
of the fact that both Beth and the baby had gone
back to sleep again, Claire had washed up and
tidied the kitchen, returned the uneaten food to
the fridge, laid the table, plus a tray for Beth,
and made a large pan of vegetable soup based as
closely as possible on her memory of a recipe
her mother had used for years. She had also laid
out bread, pickles, and cold meats, and a bowl
of fruit. Satisfied there was little else she could
do, she had then sat down and waited for them
to arrive.

One look at their faces told her all she
needed to know. It was obvious from their
expressions that they had had a bad time and
that they were tired and hungry, as well as
worried out of their wits.

"It's okay! Everything is fine," she
hastened to reassure them as they reached the
top of the stairs. "Beth and the baby are both
asleep. He's a lovely little boy," she added,
smiling at Carl.

He dumped his bag, stripped off his coat,
and disappeared into the bedroom without a

word, leaving Claire and Daniel staring at one another.

Hardening her heart against the weariness she could see on his face, Claire told him what had happened; why Beth had called her; and why the baby had ended up being born at home. Then she waved towards the food on the table, told him soup was simmering on the stove, picked up her bags, and prepared to leave.

He put out a hand to stop her. "Please don't go yet Claire. Carl will want to thank you for everything you've done. I don't even want to think about what might have happened if you hadn't been here."

"If I hadn't been here then Beth would have called someone else," Claire told him, her manner matter-of-fact. She was determined to keep emotion out of this. She was also desperate to leave before Daniel met his new nephew.

"Look I have to go. There are things I must do, things that won't wait. Give Beth my love and tell her I'll be in touch later."

He gave a slow nod. "I'll do that, but I'll also come and find you myself later on. There are things I need to say to you Claire. Things I should have told you when you first arrived in Florida."

She turned away dismissively and headed for the stairs. There was nothing he could or should have told her that would influence what she was about to do. Nor was she going to let him stop her, which was why she had to go now, before she gave herself away, and before her heart broke entirely when she saw him nursing the baby nephew who he probably wished was his own son.

* * *

She didn't give herself time to think when she reached her apartment either. She just dumped her belongings inside and called the airport and the local taxi service. Then she hurried back down the stairs and walked to the office to collect the golf cart she kept parked outside its main door. She took it without bothering to tell Scott whose head she could see through the office window.

Although it was still windy the gusts had lost most of their force. The aftermath of the storm meant it took her longer than usual to drive to the Marchant's family home, however, because the streets were strewn with broken branches and other debris. When she eventually arrived she went straight round to the rear of the house, knowing that she was most likely to find Mrs Marchant in the kitchen.

As expected, she was standing at the counter preparing a meal for later in the day. She smiled a welcome at Claire and asked her if she would like a coffee.

"Thank you, but no," Claire shook her head decisively. "I haven't really come to socialize. I need to talk to Mr Marchant about something, but before I do I have some news for you. Beth had a little boy this morning. He is completely beautiful and will probably look like Carl when his features straighten out and he stops frowning…"

She stopped abruptly as Mrs Marchant burst into tears.

"I'm sorry," she said, pushing away a feeling of guilt. "I should have realized it would be a shock and led up to it a bit more gently. They're both at home though because the storm meant Beth couldn't make it to the maternity unit. If you want to go and see them I'll stay with Mr Marchant."

For a long moment the frail woman in front of her hesitated, then she gave Claire a grateful smile. "If you really mean it, then thank you. I've already plated up some lunch for him. It's in the fridge. He usually eats around one-thirty."

"Don't worry about him. I'll make sure he knows where it is," Claire chose her words carefully as she directed her gently towards the doorway.

Mrs Marchant paused on the threshold and then turned and looked at her. "You probably think I've been a terrible coward over Carl," she said. "But coward or not, nobody is going to prevent me from seeing my first grandchild."

Then she straightened her shoulders and moved purposefully across the hallway to the main entrance and went outside. Within moments Claire heard the roar of a car engine.

She gave a grim smile of satisfaction as she set off in search of Daniel's father.

* * *

She found him in his study listening to music. When he heard her enter the room he assumed it was his wife and turned towards her with a querulous frown on his face.

"Surely it must be lunchtime by now."

"Mrs Marchant said to tell you that your lunch is on a plate in the fridge."

His frown grew fiercer when he heard Claire's voice. "What do you mean, it's in the fridge? Why hasn't she served it yet? Call her for me."

"I can't. She's not here. She's gone to see your new grandson," Claire told him. "He was born at four-thirty this morning, in his home above Carl's print shop. And if you were a better father and husband then she would have been there with Beth when she needed her. She would have been there for his birth, instead of here with you, pandering to your every whim!"

"How dare you!" Gordon Marchant put his hands on the desk and pushed himself to his feet. His face was red with anger.

"I dare because nobody else will," Claire told him coolly. "I dare because I was the one who saw your first grandchild enter the world, instead of the grandmother who would have so loved to be there. I dare because I know what your cruel words did to Beth, the woman who loves your son, the woman who has helped him back from the brink without any assistance from you."

"If you have quite finished, then I would like you to leave my house. I don't take kindly to having my hospitality thrust back in my face."

"Oh don't worry, I'm going to leave, and soon, but not until we've talked about every single thing you've destroyed, including the family business."

He sank back in his chair, the fight draining out of him at her words. "What do you mean?"

"I mean that you have driven Daniel relentlessly without once giving him any true authority over the business, without even caring if it's what he wants to do with his life. You weren't even being prepared to let Carl help him. Well now you're about to pay for your intransigence because your company is in meltdown. The only way out has been for Daniel and Carl to ask the rest of the directors to remove you from the Board. I don't know whether they've been successful. I didn't ask. What I do know, however, is that even thinking about doing it has almost broken their hearts."

She steeled herself to ignore the desperation on his face as she continued. "And as well as destroying your business, you have almost destroyed your wife. I know you can't see her, but surely you can sense how frail she is, how nervous you make her every time you lose your temper.

"And it's the same with the twins. They're frightened of you too. Melanie has a boyfriend who she loves very much, but she's afraid to tell you about him in case you say you don't think he's suitable. She thinks you might throw her out of the house, just like you did Carl."

Pausing for breath she leaned forward and rested both hands on the desk in front of him, noticing, as she did so, how his face had grown pale, and how his hands were trembling. Refusing to feel sorry for him, she began to speak again.

"When I first met you, I felt sorry for you. Losing your sight must have been a terrible blow. I knew you were grieving for all the things you could no longer do. But now I know you, now I can see that you don't ever intend to help yourself but prefer to bully everyone around you into doing your bidding without question…well, I've just stopped caring.

"You're one of the most selfish people I've ever met. You won't even do something as simple as join the Talking Books Service…something that was set up by people wanting to help. Instead you would rather sit around feeling sorry for yourself until someone, usually your poor wife, has the time to read to you.

" And you obviously haven't heard we've entered the computer age either. There is enough technology out there to bring you back into the world of work if only you could be bothered to give it a try. Ask your friend Tom

Cook. He's moved on. Oh, I forgot…you've given up on all your friends too, haven't you?"

"Enough Claire! What *do* you think you're doing?" Daniel's voice was sharp as he came up behind her. His fingers bit into her shoulders as he swung her round towards him.

"Oh don't worry, I've finished," she told him, angrily shrugging him away from her. "I've done what you should have done months ago. I'm going now. I'm sorry about the job but I can't do it any longer. Not after this. Find yourself someone who doesn't care about the fact that your father is slowly destroying your family Daniel. Find yourself someone who doesn't care about *you*!"

Chapter Twenty-One

A long spell of summer drizzle had greeted Claire when she arrived back in England. Unwilling to talk to anyone about her experiences in Florida, she had fled to her parent's house as soon as she landed, knowing they would give her the time she needed for her heart to heal. That they were concerned about her was very clear but they didn't ask questions, trusting instead that she would tell them what she wanted to in her own good time. She was immeasurably grateful for their patience, but also ashamed she was prepared to accept their unquestioning hospitality without giving anything in return.

Now, almost a month later, her interest stirred slightly as she stood looking out of the kitchen window at the early morning rays of a watery sun. Maybe she would go out. She wouldn't take her camera with her though. Carrying it was still too reminiscent of the time she had spent at Dolphin Key where, whichever way she looked, there had always been something new to photograph. Instead she would take a long beach walk and hope the fresh westerly breeze would clear away the misery that had been hounding her ever since she returned.

On a good day she was sure she had been right to behave as she did, but on a bad day she squirmed with embarrassment as she remembered everything she had said to Mr Marchant. None of it was any of her business and she should have held her tongue. She only hoped that in the end it had done a bit of good. If it had then it would have been worth it. Not that she expected to find out any time soon because she was still ignoring the messages on her cell phone and refusing to look at her emails.

The only contact she'd had with Dolphin Key since she left was to send Beth the photos she had taken of the baby. She hadn't added a message, or an explanation, because there was nothing she wanted to say. Her behavior would be sufficient explanation for Beth. She would know just why Claire had behaved as she did, and would probably condone it. The same couldn't be said for Daniel though. She remembered the harsh pressure of his fingers when they gripped her shoulders and shuddered, even while she allowed herself a bitter smile. At least she had achieved the outcome she had wanted for herself. Without planning to, she had found a way to leave Dolphin Key that ensured she would never be welcomed back. At least now she didn't need to worry about having to see Daniel Marchant ever again.

"Going out darling?" Her mother came into the kitchen clad in her usual mismatch of drapes and scarves. Today she was wearing a black and white sarong over a scarlet blouse, and she had tied her hair up with emerald green ribbons.

"I thought I might," Claire said. "Perhaps the wind will blow the cobwebs away."

"Mmm, I suppose so." Then, noticing the local paper had arrived she seemed to lose interest in Claire's dilemma. Whether the group campaigning about the proposed new supermarket had been successful with their latest petition appeared to be of much greater interest to her. She carried on flicking through it as Claire took a few items of food from the larder and threw them into a small backpack. Adding sun cream and lip salve, she pushed a pair of sunglasses up into her hair in case the sun decided to come right out instead of playing hide-and-seek behind the clouds.

"Have a good time," her mother called as Claire opened the kitchen door and stepped outside. Then, as an afterthought, she asked her where she was going.

"Probably as far as the lifeboat station," Claire told her. "I need a long walk. I've been cooped up for far too long."

"Yes, I'm sure dear. Well try to get back for the evening meal won't you, or I might start worrying."

As if, thought Claire gloomily as she trudged down towards the beach. She knew how much her parents loved her. It showed with every question they had refrained from asking since she returned home. It showed, too, in their casual cosseting, in the fact that her mother kept cooking her favourite meals, while her father brought home piles of books from the local library. Books he thought might interest her. She loved and appreciated them for it, but she knew they wouldn't worry if she were late home, because they never worried about where she was. They had always said they had far too much faith in her common sense to spend energy worrying about things that might never happen, and obviously nothing had changed.

* * *

She spent the morning mooching along the shore with her cotton trousers rolled up, kicking through the waves. It helped a little, just being back beside the sea. She tried not to mind that it wasn't Dolphin Key; that the seagulls were different; that there were fewer shells; and that she was unraveling different tangles of seaweed. And when she thought she had cleared the memories of Florida from her mind, she climbed up to the top of a sand dune and started to eat her lunch.

By the fourth mouthful she had lost her appetite though. She pushed the rest of the food back into her backpack, unscrewed a bottle of water, and took a long drink. Then she laid back and looked up at the sky through the spikes of marram grass that grew in random green tufts across the sand dunes.

She was asleep when Daniel found her. He stood for a long time looking down at her sleeping face, noticing the new hollows in her cheeks. He noticed, too, that she was more slender than when he had last seen her. With a sigh he sat down beside her and waited for her to wake up.

* * *

Claire opened her eyes when a cloud sailed across the face of the sun. She sat up with a shiver, looked round for her backpack, and found herself staring into a pair of troubled brown eyes.

"Your mother said I would probably find you near the lifeboat station." Daniel gave a half smile as he pulled her jumper from the top of her rucksack and draped it around her shoulders.

"Thank you…I…why are you here?" She pushed her arms into its sleeves and pulled the jumper over her head as she spoke.

"Because it seems to be the only way I can get you to speak to me," he told her when she re-emerged. Her hair was ruffled into the cloudy mass of curls he loved so much. "Without your mother's daily emails I would have gone mad. She has been keeping me up to date. Why haven't you answered my phone calls, or the messages I sent you?"

"Because there's nothing I want to say to you," she kept her eyes fixed firmly on a ferry that was sailing on the outgoing tide.

"You had plenty to say to my father," he reminded her. "Of course I missed most of it, but I heard enough to know you didn't have any problem with words then."

"If you are expecting me to say sorry then you are going to be very disappointed." The anger that had prompted her actions in the first place started to rekindle as she swung round to face him.

"I'm not expecting an apology Claire. I just want to understand why you ran out on me."

She glared at him. "Surely it's obvious. It was impossible for me to stay after I was so rude to your father. I broke Melanie's confidence too. I even told him what you and Carl were going to do to the business but without checking whether you had actually gone through with it. Then, to cap it all, I encouraged your mother to abandon post and go and see her new grandson. The child of the son whose name must never ever be mentioned in the Marchant family."

"Yes, I know all that, but it wasn't my question. What I asked was, *why did you run out on me?*"

His eyes didn't waiver as he waited for her answer and when surprise kept her silent he leaned forward and gently took hold of both her hands. "I can remember the exact words you used the last time you spoke to me Claire. You

253

said, *'find yourself someone who doesn't care about the fact that your father is slowly destroying your family Daniel. Find yourself someone who doesn't care about you!'* My question is, did you really mean it?"

"Yes." She looked down at their hands, to where his strong brown fingers had enclosed her own, and wondered why she had started trembling.

"I thought so." He moved one of his hands to her face and gently turned it towards him. "I've been such a fool Claire. There was so much going on in my life that I couldn't see what was in front of me until you took it away.

"I felt so guilty about persuading you to come to Florida to work when I knew all along that I had an ulterior motive, that I took too long to tell you how I felt about you. It never occurred to me that you might feel the same way. Instead I kept remembering how vehemently you had told me you weren't interested in dating anyone, so I decided to play the long game. That is until you started a relationship with Scott, at which point I lost all hope that you would ever…"

"What relationship with Scott?" Claire interrupted, her forehead furrowed into a frown until she saw the Daniel's wry smile. Then she started to laugh. "Oh, you mean that relationship!"

"Yes! The relationship he and Melanie were forced to tell me about after you blew their cover!"

"Poor Scott! He was eaten up with worry about keeping it a secret."

"Mmm. That's what he told me while I was bawling him out. He also told me I should sort out my own feelings before I criticized anyone else."

"Scott said that?"

"Yes. He was the only one who had any idea how we felt about one another. He said it was about time I did something about it instead of worrying about everybody else in Dolphin Key."

"And?"

"And so I'm here to do something about it," he told her, pulling her close. Then he kissed her.

* * *

They didn't say very much at all for a very long time after that. They might have stayed there even longer if a short-lived flurry of rain hadn't interrupted them.

"*Thank you Scott*," Daniel murmured as he stood up and pulled Claire to her feet. She grinned at him; her eyes alight with the mischief that had been missing from her face for so long.

"Does that mean he and Melanie are forgiven"

"See for yourself," Daniel thrust his hand into his pocket and pulled out his cell phone. Scrolling through the photos stored in its memory he finally found what he was looking for, and handed it to Claire.

A short video started to play. The picture was clear enough for Claire to see it had been taken outside his house. As she watched, the camera zoomed in to two people sitting close together on the dock. It was Scott and Melanie, and when they turned towards the photographer they started laughing. Then they waved directly into the camera.

"Come back Claire," they called out in unison. *"Our engagement party is on the fifteenth of next month. Please be back by then."*

"I've got a few other messages too," he told her, retrieving the camera and scrolling down.

The next one was of Beth and the baby. *"We need you back here,"* she told Claire. *"Harris wants you to see how much he's grown...and I, well I just miss you."*

"Harris!" Claire whispered, her eyes swimming with tears as she looked at Daniel.

"Mmm. Beth and Carl think it's a good name for a boy. I think they've got a certain Claire Harris earmarked to be godmother too."

"And you have come to terms with Beth being married to Carl?"

Now it was Daniel's turn to look mystified.

"You...Beth was your girlfriend until Carl came along," she reminded him, resisting the urge to look away even though she didn't want to see the memories she was sure would shadow his face. "That's why you weren't looking for anyone to date, remember. You were still coming to terms with the fact she left you for your brother."

"Where on earth did that come from?" Daniel asked, as he took the camera from her unresisting fingers and stuffed it back into his pocket. Then, when she didn't answer, he shook his head.

"Sure I went out with Beth for a while Claire, but she was never going to be the love of my life. We had fun together for half a summer and then she met Carl. Once that happened I may as well not have existed, but it was absolutely fine by me. I like Beth, love her as a friend, a sister…but that's it. The rest is a figment of your imagination. It's you I love, and I have done so since the first moment I saw you."

"But you can't love me," she sank down onto the ground again and covered her face with her hands. "I was rude to your father. I helped to hide Scott and Melanie's relationship from you, I…."

Daniel interrupted her by sitting down beside her and taking her in his arms again. "All history," he said. "Thanks to you, we didn't need to remove Dad from the Board after all, because he resigned before the final motion went through. And he says he's going to take a computer course at the end of the summer. He's joined the Talking Books Service as well. There's a message from him on my phone too. Something about thanking you for doing what

257

nobody else dared to do. Well that's what he means, even if he didn't quite put it like that," he told her with a wry smile.

"And your mother?" she lifted a tear-stained face hopefully to his.

"Is in her element helping to care for her first grandchild. She is going to help out in the print shop as well, because Carl will be too busy running the family business to spend much time there in future. And when Harris is a little older, she and Beth intend to expand it into a working art gallery, and encourage other artists to join them."

He smiled at her as he leaned forward and kissed away the last of her tears. "Of course all these changes leave me without a full time job. I'm still on the Company Board. Actually I was voted in as Chairman so I will still be involved, but only part time…so I need to find another way to earn a decent living."

"You're going to expand your own company," she said, and the smile on her face was like sunshine after a storm.

"I am. But to make it truly successful I need someone who has cataloguing skills. I also need someone who can take photographs as well as develop and run training courses. There's a vacancy for someone who can talk to the visiting public too and…most importantly…is prepared to be around twenty-four hours a day. Do you know anyone who might be interested?"

Epilogue

The boat sailing away from the Marchant's big old family home was ablaze with fairy lights. They were draped along the side rails and twisted up the poles that supported its striped canopy. A big cheer went up from the people standing on the dock, and most of them stayed where they were until the boat disappeared from view.

"That was so romantic. How lovely to get married at Christmas, and in such an idyllic setting. If I wasn't so happy with Mark then I might even feel a tiny bit jealous." Jenny and her husband followed Claire's parents back into the marquee that had been erected on the lawn.

"I didn't think much of her going away outfit though. Still I can see that things are done differently over here."

* * *

Claire, sitting at the prow of the boat, watched the house and all of their wedding guests fade from view. When they had completely disappeared she moved across to the stern and took her husband's hand off the throttle. Immediately the boat's engine slowed to a soft putter.

Daniel smiled at her. She was wearing a pink T-shirt and a matching wrap over khaki cut offs, and her feet were bare.

259

"Are you sure you don't want to go somewhere more exotic than Dolphin Key for a honeymoon?" he asked her. "It's not too late you know. We can pick up a flight to anywhere you choose in the morning."

"I'm sure," she said, snuggling up against him as a night breeze suddenly whisked up a few waves and made the boat rock gently to and fro. "I've spent too long away from it recently to want to leave now. Besides, nobody will dare to visit us for at least twenty-four hours!"

"You're confident about that are you?" he asked. There was a hint of resignation in his voice as his house came slowly into view. All the lights were blazing and they could hear music drifting across the bay.

"Completely, because I put Carl and Beth on the case," she said. "That's just their way of welcoming us home."

With a sharp intake of breath he increased their speed, only slowing down again when the boat reached the dock. With one deft twist of the rope he secured it to the mooring ring and turned off the engine. Then he bent down and kissed her hard. It was a kiss that was full of promise and it only ended when he picked her up and dumped her on the dock.

"I know that wasn't exactly a romantic move but give me time and I'll do better," he told her as he clambered up beside her. Then he swept her up into his arms again.

She locked her hands around his neck. He was taller than anyone she knew, tall enough to make her feel small. He was strong enough to make her feel fragile and protected too, despite the length of her legs and the slender curves of her body. It wasn't a feeling she was used to but it was one she was rapidly learning to enjoy.

"I'm going to love living here," she told him, kissing his cheek.

He nuzzled her ear. "You're a shameless hussy Mrs Marchant, marrying a man just for his property!"

"Oh I haven't married you just for your property," she told him wickedly as he carried her over the doorstep and into a bedroom whose windows overlooked the midnight sea. "But you *are* right about the shameless hussy bit!"

He laughed out loud then, and kicked the bedroom door shut behind him. After that it wasn't very long before the all the lights went out, and the house in the deserted cove faded into a murmuring darkness.

The End

Other Books We Love books by Sheila Claydon

Cabin Fever
Reluctant Date
Double Fault
Kissing Maggie Silver
Mending Jodie's Heart (When Paths Meet Book 1)
Finding Bella Blue (When Paths Meet Book 2)
Saving Katy Gray (When Paths Meet Book 3)
Miss Locatelli
Remembering Rose (Mapleby Memories Book 1)
The Sheila Claydon Special Edition
The Hollywood Collection

In the 1980s Sheila Claydon wrote a number of romances under the pseudonym Anne Beverley. Then a busy career and family life got in the way and before she knew it, she had turned her back on the characters who were begging to be liberated from her imagination. Now she is back to writing fiction again and, considerably older and no longer shy, writes under her own name.

262

Her motto is a quote by the late Ray Bradbury: "First, find out what your hero wants. Then just follow him."

Although family remains central to her life, she still finds the time to read, to write, and to travel. Many of the places she has visited feature in her books. Her fans say that reading them is like buying a ticket to romance.

You can find her at https://www.facebook.com/SheilaClaydon.author/